The
Music Teacher

The
Music Teacher

Robert Starer

THE OVERLOOK PRESS
WOODSTOCK • NEW YORK

First published in the United States in 1997 by
The Overlook Press
Lewis Hollow Road
Woodstock, New York 12498

Library of Congress Cataloging-in-Publications Data

Starer, Robert.
The music teacher / Robert Starer.
p. cm.
ISBN 0-87951-756-5
I. Title.
PS3569.T335645MB7   1997   813'.54—dc20   96-29263

BOOK DESIGN AND FORMATTING BY BERNARD SCHLEIFER

Printed in the United States of America

First Edition

10 9 8 7 6 5 4 3 2 1

To my friends who teach music

The
Music Teacher

Chapter **1**

WHEN LYDIA FIRST CAME TO HIS STUDIO, HER YOUNG SON at her side, Bernard thought she would ask him to teach the boy and he would have to explain to her that he did not take beginners. He dreaded those situations, knowing that mothers could not tolerate to see their children rejected, and yet he had had to do it often. His reputation as a teacher was so good that he had waiting lists and could be very selective in taking on new students.

But she had wanted to take up the piano herself. She had recently been divorced, she said; her son, Carl, now went to school all day; she had time, no need to earn money—as she put it—and she had always loved the piano, ever since childhood.

"Why don't you play something for me?" Bernard said, looking at her for the first time with interest.

"I haven't touched a keyboard for a long time," she replied, "at least not with any degree of consistency, what with the divorce and other things."

"We have to start somewhere. I have to have a notion of your ability."

"Well . . . all right."

She left her son on the couch they had been sitting on, smoothed her light blond hair, although it did not need it, and walked briskly to the Steinway. Bernard had two pianos facing each other, one for the students and one that only he himself touched. The room was arranged in such a way that even a newcomer would head for the student's instrument.

Lydia sat down, played a few notes, and stopped to adjust the piano stool. She needed to lower it. Tall girl, Bernard thought, looking at her legs, now at a more comfortable angle. He did not ask her what she was going to play; this often seemed to inhibit students at their first audition. I'll recognize it, he thought. God help me if I don't. They mostly play the same pieces anyway.

To his surprise Lydia played the opening prelude of one of Bach's English Suites, a piece dependant upon finger dexterity, and while the stiffness of her fingers made for some unevenness in the faster passages, he was impressed by the forcefulness of her playing and the conviction behind her interpretation.

"It sounds as though you really have this piece in your fingers," he said encouragingly, when she had finished.

"Well . . . I *did* practice a little, these past few days," she admitted with a girlish smile, as her shoulders lost some of their tautness. "Would you like to hear some more?"

"Yes."

She played a little rondo by Mozart, shaping each phrase with delicacy, and a Chopin prelude with a singing tone in her right hand and a well-shaded accompaniment in the left.

"Anything from our century?" Bernard asked, expecting some Debussy.

To his surprise she played several of Prokofiev's *Visions fugitives*, with the same forcefulness she had used in the Bach.

"With whom did you study?" he asked, warming up to this tall woman's playing.

"Since I began playing?"

"No, your most recent teacher."

She named a well-known Russian pianist who had lived in New York.

"A fine pianist and, to judge by your playing, a fine teacher as well. But he's been dead about ten years, hasn't he?"

"He died the year I studied with him," she answered. "Very unexpectedly. It happened exactly eight years ago. I know because it was also the year I met my husband— my ex-husband, I should say. It was when I stopped playing seriously.

"But you played all these pieces from memory. Did you look at them during those eight years?"

"No. I didn't."

"That's quite a remarkable feat, then."

"Oh, I never forget a piece of music once I've learned it."

"Do you mean you could play anything you ever learned right now, for instance?"

"I think so."

"May I test you?"

She nodded.

"How about the first Bach three-part invention?"

She played it without any hesitation, not quite up to tempo but entirely accurately.

"Schumann's *Träumerei*?"

"Oh, come on. Anybody can do that."

"Perhaps I wanted to make it a little easier for you, after that Bach. Do you know any Debussy?"

"I used to play *Pour le Piano*."

"Fine."

Again her fingers produced the first piece of that set.

"You are a rather astonishing . . . person," Bernard said, as much to himself as to her. He couldn't quite decide whether to say "girl"—she looked so young—or "woman"—she did have a school-age child. "Person" was safe these days, neutral and unobjectionable.

The same girlish smile appeared at the edges of her lips that she had shown when she admitted to having practiced for a few days before coming to see him.

Bernard did not return the smile. "Why did you come to *me*?" he asked. "We live only an hour from New York. You could go into the city and study with anyone."

"I don't want to study with *anyone*. I want to study with you."

"Very flattering," he said, "but I still don't know why."

She turned around on the piano stool and faced him directly. Her clear, light, metallic-blue eyes looked straight at him, without any guile. Her nose was short and narrow and her skin white, perhaps a little shiny but without blemishes. A small cleft in her chin gave her face an expression of determination.

Attractive, Bernard thought; not entirely likable, but certainly attractive.

"I want to study with you because I heard you play," she said. "I think you are a much better pianist than all those big 'names' that pack Lincoln Center and Carnegie Hall with their prefabricated success stories. After I heard you play last fall at the Community College, I went to the record store to buy any recordings you might have made. There weren't any on the shelves, so I asked the clerk. He looked you up in the Schwann catalog and said he could order some, but they didn't keep them in stock."

"I am well aware of that situation."

"Then I saw an announcement in the paper that you were playing a Mozart concerto with the local chamber orchestra, so I went to hear you again. I so much agreed with what you did, every nuance, that I knew if I were ever going to take up the piano again, it would have to be with you."

The boy, who had been unusually attentive during the music, had gotten restless and wriggled off the couch when they began to talk.

"Mom, when are we going home?"

"In a minute, Carl," she said, looking only at Bernard. "Please don't say there is no room in your schedule."

"I'd find room for you even if I had to kick out someone else," Bernard heard himself say with some surprise. She had gotten up, and he found he had walked over to her and was touching her upper arms lightly with his hands. She was a little taller than he, he noticed. "And thank you for what you said about my playing. It will be a pleasure to work with you." He made a slight formal bow, his arms back at his side.

Carl was coming toward them. He pulled at his mother's skirt. "I want to go home, Mom."

"I know, honey."

Bernard looked at the boy, who did not resemble his mother at all, except for the light-blue eyes. His build was stocky, his complexion swarthy, and his hair was coal-black.

She must have married someone from a Mediterranean

country, Bernard thought, perhaps a Greek or a Sicilian. For a moment he was jealous of the man who had been married to this woman for eight years. To regain distance and dignity, he walked to his desk to look at his appointment book while mother and son stood together near the piano. Lydia was holding Carl's hand in hers.

"Please sit down, Mrs. . . . . Harding," he said. "Is this your maiden or married name? I have to ask you a question, and please try to answer it truthfully: *Why* do you want to take up the piano again?"

The smile reappeared at the edges of her lips as she spoke. "To answer your questions in the order you asked them, Harding is my maiden name—my married name was long and Armenian—and I don't have any illusions about the possibility of a pianistic career at my age. I'm thirty-two, you might as well know, and the question of success and failure has been part of my daily life for the past eight years. My husband measured everyone he met by these standards. He looked up to the 'successes' and despised the 'failures.' I have no time for these considerations; I want to play the piano again because it gives me pleasure, a deeper pleasure than anything else. When I listened to your performance of that Mozart concerto with the chamber orchestra, I realized how much I had missed it."

She had gotten agitated, almost excited, as she spoke and her face had taken on a pinkish tinge. Her soft and lingering enunciation of certain words had revealed a slight southern accent.

I wonder what she would be like when she is really angry, Bernard thought, I'll probably never know.

"I like what I heard," he said, quite formally, almost pompously. "I think we will get along fine. Someday, when I know you better, we will talk about success and failure. I have some thoughts on that matter as well as some experiences. But now we must set our first appointment. Carl here is getting very restless. How about Wednesday at four?"

"Wonderful. What music do you want me to bring?"

"Let me think for a moment. We need to work on finger dexterity and technique at first. Straight playing without pedal is what I would recommend. Bring the *Well-tempered Clavier*, both volumes. I hope you have a good edition."

"I think I do, even if I can't pronounce it."

"Must be the Bach-Gesellschaft."

"You're right, it is."

As they turned to leave his apartment, the boy noticed a small, heavily ornamented metallic object nailed diagonally to the door frame.

"What is that?" he asked his mother.

She turned to Bernard questioningly.

"It is called a mezuzah," he said. "I am not sure what its function is or what it contains, perhaps the ten commandments or a Hebrew prayer. It is meant to ward off evil, and you are supposed to touch it with your fingers and then kiss them. I don't do that myself, but this mezuzah has been in my mother's family for generations and I kept it mostly to honor her memory."

Carl tried to reach it, but it was too high for him. Lydia gently led him out the door. Bernard went to the window to watch them drive away. It was early spring, and the first signs of new life were appearing on the trees, reddish-brown before turning green.

He saw Lydia secure the seat belt around Carl, firmly but lovingly, as she stroked his hair with one hand. Her gesture sent a pang through Bernard as he thought of his own mother, dead for many years. Of course there had been no seat belts when he was Carl's age, but he had no memories of his mother taking care of him with firm but loving gestures; he only remembered his taking care of her during her long periods of depression. There must have been such moments in my life also, he thought; I have just forgotten them.

Why did I take this tall woman on as a student? he questioned himself. She did play well and her musical memory is truly remarkable, but don't I work too much as it is? Just yesterday he had turned away a woman who had told him on the phone that her son was a "genius." After listening to his pallid playing he had told her that his schedule was full. What was it Rubinstein is supposed to have said in a similar situation? "Your son may be a genius, madam, but talent he has none." I wish I had had the chutzpah to say something similar to that woman.

Why had Lydia gotten so excited when she talked about her husband's obsession with success and failure? Was it because she was speaking of him—perhaps they had gone through a painful, belligerent divorce—or was it because of the subject? Aren't we all obsessed with being successes or failures? Or is it only our society, our overly materialistic society, that applies those standards as measurements of quality? Are we the only ones to call a human being—not just an event—a success or a failure?

I wonder what her husband, her ex-husband, is like? All I know about him is that he supplied the genes for Carl's black hair and dark complexion. How quiet the boy was during the music and how restless the moment it was over. She said she met her husband the year her piano teacher died. Coincidence, or more? And why was he so obsessed with success and failure?

There are many kinds of success—his thoughts ran on—

and indeed many kinds of failure. Why had he, who had loved a number of women, not succeeded in staying with anyone for more than two or three years?

Success can be measured on different levels. There is international success and there is national success. Your name can be a so-called household word everywhere or just in your town or village. Did not Julius Caesar say he'd rather be the first in a small village than the second in Rome?

Bernard, who had studied in Paris and Rome, remembered how well the French qualify the different kinds of *succès*. Aside from unqualified success they had *succès d'estime*, when people respected you but did not love you, and *succès de scandale*,when you got famous by doing something notorious. In music, he thought, Stravinsky's *Rite of Spring* must be counted in that category. Perhaps also Ravel's *Boléro*, which became famous overnight because the dancer who commissioned it appeared almost nude.

Whom else had he known in his own life who had been preoccupied with that arbitrary division of mankind? Margaret, of course—Mitzi as she liked to be called by her intimates—his former wife. Her craving for success had been almost like an illness or like an all-pervading force. And success had quite unbalanced her; she had been incapable of dealing with it. It had created in her only a hunger for more, a need to climb ever higher on the ladder of success until she had lost all perspective of other things that mattered in life. To modify a cliché: Success corrupts, and absolute success corrupts absolutely.

His thoughts returned to Lydia, whom he had just accepted as a student. What a mixture of strength and weakness she was! He remembered shaking her hand as she left. It was a soft hand, a woman's hand, yet there was a strength in it of steely bones.

He turned away from the window and looked at his apartment as it must have appeared to her. There was a small foyer, or antechamber, as he liked to call it, with a bench for students who arrived too early for their lesson. On a low table in front were music magazines and announcements of forthcoming concerts, especially piano recitals. He liked his students to read about music and what was going on in the music world, and he very much encouraged their going to as many concerts as possible. Most of them did not need his encouragement; they had enough natural curiosity and the desire to compare themselves with the achievement of others. He put on that table fliers of concerts he thought they *should* attend.

As he walked back into his studio, he mulled over where to eat supper. Lydia had been his last appointment of the day, and Bernard did not like to cook. He often ate out and then returned to an evening of solitude, of playing the piano purely for his pleasure. He had favorites that he liked to play again and again, and he also enjoyed looking at new music. Publishers always sent him what they had just brought out, and he looked at everything that came in the mail. If he liked what he saw, he gave the music to a student and got to know it intimately as they worked on it together. He had gotten into that habit with Roger, his most famous student. Roger had had an enormous appetite for new music and included some of it in all his recitals even after he had become a truly international success.

There was a photo of Roger on the wall above the piano. He was being handed a plaque after winning a major competition. It was the only photo in Bernard's studio. All the other walls were occupied with bookcases built specifically to hold music of various sizes in upright and vertical position. There was nothing anywhere to remind him of Mitzi, his wife.

Chapter 2

BERNARD WINTER HAD MET MARGARET McCLURE IN AN acoustics class at The Music School in New York. He had chosen the class because it met in the late afternoon, a time of day he rarely accomplished anything of significance—he had the most energy in the early morning—and because he thought he needed to know more about the physics of music. Margaret McClure—Mitzi, as she soon asked him to call her—had entered the large lecture hall with a thick volume of operatic arias under her arm and an umbrella hanging from below her elbow. She had stopped halfway down the room, looked in all directions slowly and deliberately, and then chosen to sit beside Bernard.

Her entrance was noticed by everyone: the assuredness of her walk, the way she seemed to assess everyone present in terms of potential interest or usefulness, and because of her striking looks. Her hair was thick, a dark blond. You could tell that it was real, because her rich eyebrows were the same color. Her face was wide, lightly tanned, with dark eyes and strong features; her body, full without sagging. Bernard's response to her entrance was quite physical, even more so when she sat beside him and their thighs touched. There was flesh on them, soft, caressable flesh, not just bones and muscle. This immediate physical response to her presence never diminished for him, not even during their most trying periods, years later, or after long separations. It always came back, as strong as the first time, whenever he touched her, or even just saw her.

The instructor in the acoustics class was a bumbling fellow—later Bernard was told that the school had really hired him because he was a good recording engineer—who kept talking about the architecture of different concert halls and opera houses, the materials they had been built with, and how some of them had needed many changes after they were finished, all matters of little interest to Mitzi, who soon began to write notes on little scraps of paper and pass them to Bernard. Whenever she wanted his attention, she would touch him lightly just above the knee. It embarrassed him, but she seemed to enjoy it and continued more forcefully when he tried to pay attention to a comparison between the sounds inside Covent Garden and the Staatsoper in Vienna.

The instructor noticed them and asked what was going on. Before Bernard thought of a response, Mitzi had risen from her seat. "I am sorry, sir, if I disturbed you," she said. "I was only asking my neighbor the name of the opera house in Milan—it totally slipped my mind—because I meant to ask you why you had not referred to it in your discussion."

The instructor, not much older than his students, was instantly mollified and spoke at length about the acoustics of La Scala. Mitzi sat down, a victorious grin on her face as she

turned to Bernard, who was still enmeshed in her deep, full
speaking voice, which he had just heard for the first time. It
was clear to him, as it was to everyone else in the room, that
this voice would fill any concert hall or opera house without
effort or amplification. Bernard was also startled by the quick-
ness of her lie and how smoothly it had gained the sympathy
of the instructor, who from this point on often turned to her
with questions, particularly those that demanded more than
yes or no for an answer.

After class they slowly drifted toward the school's cafeteria in the basement. In the elevator she stood so close to him
that their thighs touched again. Once seated at one of the
cafeteria's bare tables with cups of coffee in front of them, she
began telling him about herself.

"I am a singer," she began, "passionately in love with
opera."

He nodded.

"I live in New Jersey, just the other side of the bridge,
and I come to town three times a week for my voice lesson,
coaching sessions, and whatever theory courses the school
offers." She added, with a sideways glance at him, "I think I
am a little older than you. I should also tell you that I am married. My husband is a dentist, and we have two little girls."

"I'd love to hear you sing." He meant it.

"I'll tell you what. Let's find an empty practice room and
go over some of the arias in this volume. I know you are a
pianist. Have you done any accompanying?"

"Not much, but I'd love to make a little music with you."

As was the custom at the music school, they opened doors
to practice rooms until they found an empty one. She put her
volume of arias on the piano and opened it to a dog-eared
page. Bernard knew the music, and she sang it with her full

21

voice without any warm-up. She took many liberties with the music, but he followed her with ease.

"You played that well," she told him.

After a few more arias, most of them well-known pieces Bernard had at least heard, she leaned over the top of the piano and looked at him with a wistful smile.

"I like your piano playing. I like it very much. It is very masculine—but then, so are you."

Suddenly she looked at her watch.

"Oh, my God, I should have been home an hour ago!"

"What will you do?"

"I'll call and tell them I'm delayed."

"You can do that from my room; I live just around the corner from here. Most of the pay phones in this place don't work anyway."

They walked a few blocks to Bernard's tiny apartment on the fifth floor of a plain brick building overlooking the elevated subway, which came out of a tunnel just below his window. It consisted of a single room with a flowery sofa that could be converted to a bed and an upright piano with a large worn rug draped over its soundboard, clearly meant to muffle the sound. There was a small table with an open newspaper and an unwashed plate on it. As they entered the room a train was on the elevated section of the subway, and they had to wait for it to disappear in the tunnel before they could resume conversation.

"Noisy, isn't it?"

"You get used to it."

Mitzi dialed a number and explained to what must have been a housekeeper or baby-sitter that she would not be home for a while. She left instructions for dinner and settled on Bernard's flowery sofa. He sat down next to her so they could touch again, seemingly by accident. She did not object.

"Nice enough place for a guy like you living alone: small, but it has all you really need. I have never lived alone," she continued. "I went straight from my parents' home to my husband's. I got married my last year in high school. This may sound like a bad joke, but it really happened: I went for prolonged dental treatment, and before it was over we got married. We had to."

Bernard was thinking that she told him so much about herself without asking him anything, when her hand was suddenly on his fly, undoing it expertly.

"You do like me, don't you?"

There was no denying it, and by removing only what was absolutely essential they made love vehemently on the unmade couch. Afterward they took off the rest of their clothes, pulled out the bed, and got acquainted with each other's body more leisurely.

"I'd better call home again," she said.

This time her husband answered the telephone.

"Sorry to be so late. Is everything all right?"

The reply was lengthy, and she played with the hair on Bernard's chest while listening to it. Then it was her turn.

"Why am I so late? The opera department is rehearsing *The Marriage of Figaro*, Carlo is directing, and he is so exciting to watch. I'm learning a great deal from just observing. You don't mind? Good. It'll go on for another hour or so. Please have Gerda put the girls to bed and give them an extra kiss from me."

It had seemed tantalizingly wicked to him at the time, more adventuresome than anything he had previously encountered. He still read about her in the papers every now and then, reports from major opera houses all over the world, but some of the comments were not entirely laudatory anymore. Just recently he had read a reviewer who stated bluntly that her best days were over, her voice had acquired a shrill overtone, and, most damning of all, she had become too stout for the part of a young girl. The critic, a woman, had also commented that her hair had remained exactly the same color.

Bernard did not like to linger on the memories of his later years with Margaret—he always thought of her as Margaret now, rather than as Mitzi—but he often thought with pleasure of their early days together, their clandestine meetings and trysts. He had been the winner then, and the dentist husband was the loser, as he had slowly displaced him in Mitzi's affection. Perhaps she had never cared much for the dentist. He was surprised, though, that she did not show any reluctance in having to part from her two little girls.

"I want to sing opera, Bernard. Opera—do you hear?—and nothing else. Nothing else matters to me."

She pursued her career with enviable energy, thought Bernard, whose own progress into the world of professional music proceeded much slower. But then, she was truly remarkable; her voice stood out noticeably everywhere.

While only a third-year student doing a major role in one of the school's productions, she was picked out by the manager of a provincial but substantial opera company to appear there in several roles the following season.

"I can't sit still for a moment, I am so excited," she said, when she came to Bernard's apartment that evening with her news. "I just have to dance with joy."

They danced, their dance gradually became an embrace , and they ended up, as they knew they would, making love on

The music teacher

the couch. When Margaret was elated—in high gear, as she called it—the only thing that calmed her down was passionate, almost violent lovemaking to the point of exhaustion. Only then could she fall asleep.

She did not call New Jersey at all that night; she never even thought of it, and that led to her eventual divorce from the dentist, a divorce she did not contest. She was glad when he asked for and got custody of the two children.

"I won't miss them," she said. "Some children are interesting, some are not. My two girls were rather dull, I am afraid. I guess they took after their father. Anyway, I don't want to be encumbered by anything."

Bernard played for her, coached her in the new parts she was learning, checked her memorization, and accompanied her wherever she went, neglecting his own practicing and study. One day, after a long rehearsal, she came to his apartment late at night and announced that she was pregnant.

"Then we must get married," Bernard had said.

"Not necessarily. There are other ways of dealing with the situation."

It was not only highly illegal in those days but also often dangerous, since few respectable doctors performed this operation.

"Even if we didn't want it," Bernard argued, "it is now a living being and we must act accordingly."

Bernard was living on a small allowance his uncle in Cincinnati was sending him, and he considered approaching him for an increase, although the uncle would surely argue that Bernard was too young to tie himself down and that it would hinder his musical career. He decided not to risk rejection by the uncle, and they got a marriage license the next morning. They told no one at first and just had a bottle of

25

champagne by themselves after returning from city hall, where a bored clerk had declared them husband and wife.

Margaret moved into his small apartment; her alimony payments ceased—the dentist must have been greatly relieved to see her married again so soon—but that did not matter; she was beginning to earn sizable fees for her appearances. When she sang with an opera company or as soloist with an orchestra, Bernard traveled with her; when she sang with only a piano as accompaniment, he played for her and earned the considerably smaller fee of an accompanist.

Then came that telegram from a German opera house, asking her to substitute for a famous diva who had been taken ill.

"How can you?" Bernard asked. "You are four months pregnant."

"But to appear at the Hamburg opera is a once-in-a-life-time chance for a young singer."

They argued back and forth without resolving anything and finally went to bed, although neither of them slept much that night.

Two days later, while Bernard was practicing in preparation for a competition at their school—the winner was to play a concerto with the orchestra—a very pale Margaret walked into their apartment. There were bloodstains on the lower half of her dress. She walked slowly to the couch and fell on it.

"My God! What have you done?"

"Can't you guess?"

"Margaret, you haven't?"

"Yes. I had to."

She was bleeding profusely and he rushed her to a nearby clinic, where the resident doctor kept her for a few hours, muttering about butchers under his breath. The bleeding stopped eventually and she was allowed to go home, her skin pale, almost white, and her body weak.

The next few days were very quiet at their apartment. No music of any kind was made and few words were spoken. Three days later she was gone. There was a note on the table: *I'm off to Hamburg. Our joint account is somewhat depleted, but I'll replenish it soon.*

A week later came a long telegram with detailed quotes from her reviews. There was no doubt: She had had an overwhelming success.

The day her telegram arrived was also the day Bernard had to play in the finals of the concerto competition. He had survived the preliminaries with ease, the semifinals with a shade more effort. Now only he, a tall lanky boy from Oklahoma with long thin fingers, and a red-haired, freckled, muscular young woman from Israel were left in the finals.

Shall I move to Hamburg with her? Bernard wondered as he played the slow movement of the concerto. What will I do there? What if another opera house wants her the following month? But if I don't go to Hamburg, she may never come back to me. Am I willing to risk that?

When his mind returned to the music, he found himself playing the final chords of the movement. His fingers had continued playing, like those of a well-programmed robot, without a controlling mind. It must have been noticeable, though, because he heard a member of the jury say, "Thank you, Mr. Winter."

At the end of the second movement? Why didn't they let me finish the concerto?

"Thank you very much, Mr. Winter," the voice said again, louder this time. Bernard got up and returned to the waiting room. Later it was announced that the young man from Oklahoma had won.

"Competitions are like lotteries," Bernard told his students nowadays. "You have to enter them if you want to have a career, but you must never expect to win." He encouraged his better students to enter as many contests as possible. It was the only quick way to prominence if you had neither money nor influential friends. "Why do you need money?" some of the more naive students would ask, as if the world were so arranged that the best got to the top by virtue of the simple fact that they were the best.

"In order to be noticed," Bernard would explain, "you *have* to give a recital, a so-called debut recital. That costs money. You must rent a hall, print programs, and, if you can afford it, advertise; otherwise no one will be there to hear you. As to influential friends: If you want to audition for an important conductor, for instance, only somebody who knows him well can arrange that. To write him yourself will at best get you a letter from his secretary saying he is too busy."

Only Roger, his most successful student, whose photo hung in his studio, had won a major competition, one Bernard himself had entered several times many years earlier without even getting to the finals. Winning that competition had been the beginning of Roger's career, since it brought not only prestige and a money prize but also appearances with major orchestras and a recording contract. Bernard was proud of Roger, never jealous; it was as if your son had attained what you could not achieve. Roger had remained on close and friendly terms with Bernard, always mentioned him in his biographical sketches, and often said in interviews that he owed everything to Mr. Winter, his only teacher.

Bernard did win one competition, a not-very-well-known

one in Italy. While Mitzi was singing with a provincial French opera company, he had obtained a traveling fellowship to Europe. To be near her he had gone to Paris, but he did not take well to the musical life of that city. He found the orchestras undisciplined, the audience snobbish, and the critics corrupt. He and his piano teacher, Mlle. Boulanger, did not agree on anything musical, and he did not fit into the circle around her to which so many young American music students gravitated. Since he had no interest in composition, he saw no point in doing endless harmony exercises under the supervision of a domineering woman.

During a soiree at the "Boulangerie," as his fellow students called it, he decided to leave Paris and continue his studies in Italy. After a three-day visit with Mitzi, spent in a large, creaking double bed except for meals, he arrived in Rome and loved the city and its life instantly. People moved as quickly as they did in Paris, drivers were as selfish and as rude, but there was something sunny about their behavior, as though nothing really mattered. While he had found Paris oppressive and sinister, he loved Rome and the Romans without any reservations.

When cheated at the grocery or at the post office—a government institution, after all—he just smiled and found it charming. When he later told his students about what goes on at a Roman post office, they did not find it so delightful. As Americans they accepted corruption at the upper level of the bureaucracy as a fact of life but expected lower-level employees to be scrupulously honest. Not so in Italy. The incident Bernard liked to relate was that when he handed an airmail letter to the clerk at the post office, the man weighed it and asked Bernard for 2,000 lire, but after collecting the money he put only a 1,000-lire stamp on the letter. This happened on several occasions; therefore, Bernard assumed it was common practice. Italian friends told him that government employees were so underpaid they had to perform such tricks to survive.

The competition Bernard won was held in a small town in the foothills of the Alps. The place totally enchanted him with its cobblestone pavements, its little houses perched on top of hills, and its enormous number of churches, surely in excess of the needs of the population. Other contestants came from different countries—though not Russia or China in those days—and a friendly spirit of camaraderie reigned. A word here and there in another language—there was always someone ready to translate—and, more importantly to Bernard, none of the mercilessly fierce competitiveness that characterized contests at his school in New York had traveled to the Italian countryside.

He even ran into people he knew: the red-haired Israeli girl who had been in the finals with him when the tall Oklahoman had won and a very intense young piano student he had met in Paris. Ronit, the Israeli girl, was highly pleased to see him.

"How very, very nice," she said, almost like an Englishwoman. "Did you come all the way from New York for this?"

"No, I was in Europe anyway. I have a traveling fellowship."

"How nice for you. Where are you spending it?"

"In Rome, of course"—as though it had been his first choice—"how about you?"

"I'm on my way home to Tel Aviv, and I thought I'd stop here. I had no idea it would be so pretty."

"Isn't it, though."

Soon the endless waiting and playing began. Contestants were given an identification number, posted outside the building, and were known only by that number until the end of the competition. Preliminaries, semifinals, and, at last, the finals. Bernard had gotten into the finals; so had Ronit and a high-strung French boy who had not fraternized with anyone. He looks as though he will commit suicide if he doesn't win, thought Bernard.

For the finals you played almost an hour, and much of it was music of your own choice. Bernard, whose taste ran to the serious, played a late Beethoven sonata and Prokofiev's seventh, which had just recently become known in the West. He was in a thoroughly elated mood, he knew not why. Nothing seemed to hold him, and he could soar as high as he wanted. Perhaps because this contest did not matter, perhaps because he had not fretted and worried about it for months; in any event, he played his very best that afternoon and was not even surprised when it was announced that he had won.

Ronit, who beneath her energetic gesticulations was a sweet-tempered girl, took him out for an evening of celebrations. She was truly happy for him. First they climbed the hill behind the largest church, where they kissed gently. Then they went to the best restaurant in town, situated on the main piazza, and ate a multi-course meal while looking at the fountain, which had little boys with tiny penises that spewed water. They drank several bottles of the strong red wine of the region and ended drowsily in Ronit's bed.

The next morning Bernard was full of remorse. It was not just the hangover, although he certainly had one. While he did not see his wife often, he had never been unfaithful to her, never even tempted to be. What did marriage mean to him? To most people, he thought, marriage meant living together, making a home together, and perhaps having children and raising them. He had never lived with Mitzi except in those first hectic days in his little room, which they spent either in bed or at the piano. They had never made a home together, and after that bloody abortion, which had shocked him so deeply at the time, there had never been even talk of a future family. Pregnancy was clearly to be avoided. And yet, he wanted to stay married; he was still attracted to her and enjoyed making music with her. Did winning a competition give him license to absolute freedom?

Ronit had no such problem. All she wanted was a big breakfast, not just the dry roll Italians seemed to find adequate, and Bernard cajoled the waiter into bringing them boiled eggs, cottage cheese, and a fresh vegetable salad, the sort of thing Ronit told him Israelis liked to begin the day with. The night before had just been a pleasant episode to her—one she would never forget, she assured him—but now she needed to look up train schedules to continue her journey.

Her attitude cheered Bernard up a little, but as soon as she had left his mood of guilt and melancholy returned. Even in those young years he knew, both from his own ups and downs and from having watched his mother, that periods of elation are almost always followed by their opposite. When he became depressed, he retreated totally into himself, did not speak, and moved as little as possible, as his mother had done. But aside from his own low feelings, he also had to consider those of another human being, his wife, to whom he had been so easily unfaithful. He decided to write her and confess everything.

He took one of those thin sheets of paper Europeans use for airmail correspondence out of the hotel drawer and addressed the envelope with its red and blue stripes to Mme. Margaret Winter—she used his name; it sounded more continental European than McClure, she said—at the opera house in Lyons.

Dear Mitzi, he began, *I have two important things to tell you.* (At least I didn't say, I have good news and bad news for you, my dear.) *I have actually won a competition, and I have . . .*

How to phrase his confession? If he described it as a casual escapade, it would show that his love for her was not strong enough. If he told her he had fallen in love, why had he made no effort to keep the girl or follow her? Perhaps he shouldn't tell her at all? In the end he decided to tell her the truth— how typical for me, he thought—that it had happened under the influence of alcohol and in the exultation of victory.

He asked the hotel to mail the letter and took the next train back to Rome. A few days later he had a short note from Mitzi. *Dear Bernard*, she said, *you worry too much. I have been sleeping with the baritone in our company for months. Now at least we are even.* She did not mention his having won the competition.

Why could he not get Mitzi out of his mind, not even now, after all those years? They had stayed married after that double confession, one so easy, one so hard, but did not see each other often. He returned to America; she stayed in Europe. Her physical attraction for him continued with all its force on the few occasions when they met. When they were not together, she appeared frequently in his dreams, not always in pleasant circumstances.

That funny little competition in Italy: There was one more thing he remembered about it. One member of the panel of judges had been a former teacher of Bernard's in New York. "Always find out who is on the jury when you enter a contest," he told his students nowadays. "It might make all the difference." A friend of his had been on the jury when Roger won, but surely that had nothing to do with Roger's victory. Roger's talent was so patently superior that he would have risen to the top even if he had not won that time, only more slowly. Bernard wished for another student like Roger, young, unspoiled, and with a potential that he could help realize.

His appointment book was open to the last Wednesday in March. Today at four that tall Lydia Harding is coming, the one with the handsome boy. How nice. He thought of her legs, her eyes, and her remarkable memory. What a combination! I wonder whether she will bring the boy again.

She came alone, promptly at four. They worked on the "fingery" preludes in volume one of the *Well-tempered Clavier*. Bernard checked the position of her hands and showed her where her playing had been sloppy.

"We'll get you back into shape right quickly," he said, humorously trying to drawl out the last words the way she would do.

"Now, don't you make fun of me, Mr. Winter. Besides, *you* have an accent too, but I can't quite place it."

"I was born in Germany, but I came here as a child."

"Where in Germany?"

"A small town in the Rhineland; you won't have heard of it."

Bernard, who did not speak about himself easily, quickly turned the questioning around.

"You are from the South, though?"

"Yes, I am. From South Carolina."

"And what brought you to this area?"

"I wanted to improve my piano playing."

"And did you?"

"Until I met my husband. Then he took over my life."

"Where is your boy—isn't his name Carl?—today."

"With a neighbor."

"He's a good-looking child, but quite different from you. That came out slightly wrong. I meant good-looking in a way different from you."

"Oh, that's okay. I know exactly what you mean. He looks very much like his father, who is devastatingly good-looking. He's so good-looking that people stare after him on the street and in restaurants. Women, men, children, even animals find him attractive." Suddenly a bitter tone crept into her voice, the same tone she had used when describing her husband's dividing humanity into winners and losers.

"He also has all the drawbacks of a handsome man," she went on. "He's vain, self-centered, and convinced that everything must go his way. He still doesn't understand why I'm no longer with him. He probably never will. But he certainly is good-looking."

"Well, at least that's a problem I don't have."

"But you *are* handsome, Mr. Winter, in your own way. You have a strong face. Women prefer that to prettiness in a man."

"Well, well. Let's get back to Bach."

Chapter 3

THE BOY WHO TOOK HIS LESSON RIGHT AFTER LYDIA WAS about sixteen years old, bony, wiry, and intense. He wore thick glasses and always came to his lesson in a white shirt and a thin black tie. He liked very early music and some of the more complex composers of the twentieth century and despised composers like Chopin and Liszt, whom he called superficial, showy, and fit only for the salon. "And since we don't have salons anymore," he would argue with Bernard, "their music should no longer be played."

"While you are a student," Bernard would insist with the sternest voice he could summon, "you will play every kind of music from every period of music and by every important composer. Later, when you are fully grown up and on your own, you can make your choices and eliminate what seems alien to your temperament. But not while you are here with me."

"But the stuff bores me."

"That may be lack of understanding on your part, an inability or unwillingness to see the values in the music of those composers. Above all, please remember that it is a performer's function—indeed, his duty—to present whatever he plays with his fullest conviction. While you play a piece, Harrison, you must believe in it. Otherwise you cannot convince an audience."

"I suppose that's true."

"It is indeed. Now let me ask you a question: If the manager of the Philharmonic were to call you one day and ask you to play a Rachmaninoff concerto with his orchestra, would you turn him down and say, 'Sorry, I only play Bach and Schoenberg'?"

"I guess not."

"I am glad you have that much common sense."

His last student that afternoon was a pimply girl with enormous breasts, no hips, and very little self-confidence. She was neither pleasant nor in any way attractive, and Bernard, who had to force himself to be kind to her, often wondered why he had kept her as a student.

She played surprisingly well that afternoon, though, and Bernard was glad he could tell her so. She liked dreamy music of an improvisatory nature, and her favorite composers were Schumann and Debussy. When Bernard, strong in his beliefs, forced some Bach on her now and then, she always said "ugh" when he assigned it and played it with visible resentment the following lesson.

"The stuff is so dry and cerebral," she would say. "I don't see any greatness in these dreary, endless fugues Mr. Johann Sebastian"—as she liked to call him—"is so respected for. It's just the same dull motif coming once on top, once in the middle, and then at the bottom or the other way around."

"There's more to a fugue than that. What about its architectural structure?"

"I don't see it. Anyway, music should come from feelings, not from the mind."

Bernard was too tired to try to convince her that only a successful combination of both elements made for great art and let her go home, assigning her a prelude by Scriabin that was more dissonant than she liked but still dreamy enough to fit into her scheme of things. He knew that arguing with her would be useless, and he also wanted to be alone and think at leisure about Lydia. How curious she was! Few students ever asked him anything about himself, certainly not in their first lesson, and he did not encourage that sort of talk. Lydia had actually paid him a compliment, quite unexpectedly, and her eyes had told him that she meant it.

Here I am, almost fifty years old—he was actually forty-eight—and still worried about whether I am attractive to women. I am not handsome, no matter what she said, but we are all vain enough to like to hear that sort of thing, even if we truly don't believe it. Bernard's father had had an endearing nickname for him in German, "my little ugly." Perhaps that had been the foundation upon which his conviction of his own ugliness rested. Men he considered good-looking were often homosexual.

And then she had noticed his trace of an accent. Bernard was not aware of it himself—is anyone ever?—and was always surprised when people mentioned it to him. Very few did, perhaps out of politeness. Bernard was only four years old when he came to America with his parents, just before the outbreak of World War II in Europe. His schooling had been in English, but his parents continued to speak German at home. They never stopped thinking of themselves as refugees and made little effort to become part of their new country.

Bernard's father, Jewish and an active Social Democrat, had spent a year in Dachau concentration camp before his wife's relatives in Cincinnati had provided the Winter family with an affidavit of support that got them an immigration visa to the United States and secured his father's release from the camp. Bernard had been too young to remember any of this, but he had heard often enough while growing up in New York how his father's health had been ruined during that year in Dachau. Even then—before the war and long before the "final solution" had been decided upon—a prolonged stay in a camp for political offenders was debilitating. Political prisoners were treated much worse than criminal offenders, not unlike in Russia.

Bernard's mother came from an old Jewish family that had lived in the same province of Germany since the fifteenth century. There were paintings of ancestors in quaint attire through all the intervening centuries, and they all had the same high, protruding cheekbones Bernard had. These ancestors had been *Hofjuden*, "court Jews," who had handled the money matters of their count or baron. No wonder the branch of his mother's family that emigrated to the United States in 1848 and settled in Cincinnati had quickly amassed wealth. Handling money had, after all, been a family tradition for generations. Luckily for the Winters, one of them, Uncle William or Willie, an old bachelor, had kept in touch with the members of the family who had stayed in Germany. He had the wisdom during the late thirties to foresee what Hitler might eventually do as well as the compassion to offer the money needed to save those members of his family who wanted to come to America.

Not all of them did. Some of them, especially those who
had served as officers in the Kaiser's army in World War I or
had held high positions in his government, simply did not
believe, not even in 1938, that this National Socialist regime
would last in their country, which to them had seemed the
most civilized and advanced in the world. Their Germany,
the land of *Dichter und Denker* (poets and thinkers)—the
Austrian Karl Kraus turned it into *Richter und Henker*
(judges and hangmen)—the country that had produced
Goethe, Heine, Nietzsche, and Beethoven, would surely not
follow that slightly ridiculous corporal from Austria much
longer. They probably died believing that.

Bernard's parents did have the sense to grasp Uncle
Willie's offer and brought their young son to New York where
they settled in the Washington Heights section of Manhattan,
near its northern tip, among all the other German-Jewish
refugees. Washington Heights was nicknamed the "Fourth
Reich" in those days, Hitler's Germany being the Third. The
area had become Hispanic, but in his childhood Bernard
heard more German spoken than English, not only at home
but also when he went shopping with his mother to the
neighborhood stores, which were owned by German-Jewish
refugees and catered almost exclusively to them.

His father had owned a textile factory in Germany but
had neither the capital—the factory had been confiscated by
the Nazis when he was interned—nor indeed the strength or
energy to start his own business again in the New World. He
went to work for others and learned English quickly because
he had to. Bernard did not begin to speak English until he
entered first grade, and his mother never accepted the new
language. Later, when she had her long periods of depression,
she spoke German if she spoke at all. Thus Bernard had kept

up his German well into his teens, which must have left the trace of an accent that Lydia had detected. Perhaps one can never quite get rid of an accent. In fact, one of his teachers had encouraged Bernard not only not to try to lose it but to consciously cultivate it. "Americans expect an artist to have an accent," he had said. "Don't lose yours. It'll do you good some day."

Uncle Willie had made it very clear that while he considered it his duty as a relative to give his distant German cousins an affidavit of support, he would not actually support them after they arrived. He had also hinted that he saw no need for them to meet face-to-face. Bernard, while on tour, had once spent a day and a night in Cincinnati and had looked Uncle Willie up in the phone book but did not call on him, honoring an ungiven promise.

Yet Uncle Willie had been enormously helpful when, soon after Bernard's father had died, his mother had had to be committed to a hospital because her depressions and hallucinations had become an almost permanent state, with only few clear periods between them. Uncle Willie had insisted that she not be sent to a state institution, where she would have lost all her civil rights, but offered to pay for her stay at a private clinic at considerable cost to himself, and he also offered to pay for Bernard's college education. Perhaps he only responded to people in deep trouble. Bernard never found out. Uncle Willie was not exactly enthusiastic when he heard that "Bernie"—he was the only person ever to call Bernard that—wanted to go to a music school, even the most famous one in the country.

Why don't you take up a profession with secure income, stability, and respectability? he asked in a letter, which also offered to introduce "Bernie" to the uncle's friends in banking and accounting. But when Bernard replied that for him music was the only thing worth living for, he did not withdraw his offer.

Bernard's recollections of his childhood centered on the small room in the Washington Heights apartment in which he had spent so many years. Its only window opened to an airshaft, and since the apartment was on the third floor of a relatively tall building, he could not tell what time of day it was by looking out that window. The room held only his narrow bed, a desk with a gooseneck lamp on a metal base, and the slightly beat-up Blüthner upright his parents had brought with them—every good middle-class German family had at least an *upright* piano—which had been placed in his room because there was no space in what served as living-dining room to the family.

That piano had been the only substantial toy, so to speak, in his room, and he began to play with it, literally with it rather than on it, when he was very small. His mother did not like the sounds he made—she called them noises—but his father, when he was at home, let him prevail. He tried to play songs he had heard and tunes that came repeatedly over the radio, struggling and correcting himself till they seemed right. As the years went by, it must have begun to sound more and more like music, and his mother stopped complaining about noises. Once he tried to tell her that the piano helped him when he felt sad or lonely and that it might do the same for her, but she did not listen to him.

A music-loving teacher in third grade encouraged him, but he had no real piano lessons until he was in junior high. One of his teachers there, a young woman from the Bronx, offered to work with him on the piano after school hours. There was another boy his age, named Peter, who loved music, and they took their lessons at the same time and then walked home together; they lived only two blocks apart. Soon they became close friends and spent all their free time playing for each other, correcting each other, and talking about pieces of music they loved or arguing about them when their tastes went in different directions.

Peter lived in a large sunny apartment, with an older sister and a much larger weekly allowance than Bernard. He was aware of political and economic developments and seemed altogether to know more about the world that surrounded them. It was he who put the first cigarette into Bernard's mouth and lit it for him. Bernard hated the taste but did not admit it, even to himself, and gradually began to enjoy the slight dizziness the first puffs of each cigarette induced in him. Now there were two reasons for him to look forward to the after-school meetings with Peter, but in retrospect he was convinced that the basis of their friendship was the piano and not the cigarettes.

Washington Heights was un-American enough not to consider love of classical music effeminate, and since Peter and he were good at sports, though not fanatically devoted to a particular one, they were not ridiculed for spending so much time with their music. They liked to play four-hand music together, and every time their bare elbows touched, as occasionally happens when playing four-hand music on one piano, Bernard felt a pleasant tingle in his whole body. He still remembered the feeling. Did he have an adolescent crush on that boy? Probably, but it all came to an end soon when Peter's family moved to California. After an exchange of three or four letters, all contact between the two boys stopped and Bernard's interest was soon transferred to a slender girl named Ruth, although she never knew about it. She was a quiet girl who did not participate in communal activities. Bernard liked to be near her, but he never spoke to her. Yet he enjoyed thinking about her and the mystery she represented to him. Boys who grow up alone know very little about girls, what they are like physically. Boys who have sisters know much more. Peter had often watched his sister undress—she had liked to do it when he was present—and he had, in return, shown her his "equipment," as he told Bernard with a foolish giggle. Bernard had to wait till he was almost eighteen before he saw and touched a girl's body—his first encounter was with another classmate, not Ruth—and he considered that to be the reason why women remained somewhat mysterious to him to this day. But he preferred that to treating sex as a physical exercise, like working out with a machine, only with a human partner.

Part of the mystery, the part that never diminished, was meeting and getting to know another human being, slowly unraveling the habits and defenses they had built around themselves to keep themselves warm and protected. He thought of Lydia, who had been to his studio a few hours earlier, and wondered why she aroused his curiosity. It is said of some men that they are attracted to ever younger replicas of the same woman again and again, but this was not true of Bernard. The women in his life had been quite different from each other and there was no one who resembled Lydia in the slightest.

So far he knew little about her. He knew her age, that she had been born in the South, and had been married to an extraordinarily handsome man. Handsome men often married bland women, he thought, to shine more themselves. But this was not the case here. Lydia was anything but bland. She disliked her ex-husband's categorizing people only into successes and failures, but perhaps she now detested all his opinions. She had never mentioned his name, only that it was long and Armenian. Had she been in love with his looks? That would not have lasted eight years. Perhaps he had had an overpowering physical hold on her, similar to Mitzi's over him.

They did have a child together, that boy who looked so much like his father. Looking at such a creature who is partly you and partly the other must create a bond between a man and a woman that holds them strongly even after they separate. Some gesture of the child, some look or expression, must remind you of the other even if he is no longer present. Is this true or are these simply the speculations of a childless man?

Bernard began to look forward to Lydia's lessons. It was a new experience for him to work with a woman in her thirties, clearly talented, an attractive woman who had interrupted her musical development to marry, raise a child, and eventually leave her husband to return to the piano. His interest in her was not entirely musical, he had to admit to himself, and yet the interest—the attraction, if you will—was quite different from the sheer physical excitement he had felt when touching Mitzi's thigh in the elevator. Perhaps that can happen only once in one's life, he thought, when you are very young and overwhelmed by the newness of the experience, when your life is governed by your glands, as a friend of his had put it. His marriage had not lasted, of course; neither had Lydia's. Does one look for other values in people later in life?

Chapter 4

THAT NIGHT BERNARD TOOK HIS FRIEND GEORGE AND HIS wife, Nancy, to dinner; they had just spent two weeks on the coast of Maine, where George liked to go to paint seascapes. George had always painted nature scenes no matter what the fashion of the day was. During the years of abstract expressionism he had tried to give his trees and lakes more geometrical outlines but had never covered them up beyond recognition. Now that the pendulum had swung back, George was called a pioneer for doing what he had done all his life anyway.

Bernard envied painters the physicality of their life: stretching canvases, mixing paints, even cleaning up. All he ever had to do to begin work was to lift the lid of his piano. Other painters Bernard had known were best in silence, but George liked to talk about his art and to ask questions about Bernard's. Once George had asked him about modulation. "I keep reading about it," he said, "but I have really no idea what it is. Is it something like a gradual change of colors?"

"In a way it is, although keys and colors are not the same thing. Rather than give you a long theoretical explanation which would not help you anyway, let's find out whether you hear a modulation. That really does matter."

Bernard had gone to the piano and begun playing in a major key and then shifted fairly abruptly into another, higher key, this time in the minor. George's eyes lit up at the right moment and he said, "Oh, that's called modulation? I have been aware of it all my life."

"Let me give you another example." This time Bernard switched almost unnoticeably from one major key to another, yet it did not escape George at all. "You subtle beast," he said. "You thought you could fool me."

"Not fool you, just test how refined your ear is. You passed with flying colors."

"Flying colors, huh!"

George's wife had sat quietly during the whole scene and then said, "So it's something you feel rather than understand." The evening had ended in a lengthy discussion of whether perception of artistic meaning is better achieved through the senses or the mind. Over a glass of fine brandy they had agreed that the two were inseparable.

When George and Nancy arrived at Bernard's apartment they first had a drink there, as they usually did, before going out to eat.

"How was your vacation in Maine?" he asked.

"Horrid," Nancy came back quickly. "It rained the whole time."

"You poor things."

47

"It wasn't all that bad," George interjected. "We stayed at an old inn. It had a large fieldstone fireplace. I arranged the logs in different positions and painted them, a new experience for me but not at all bad. Above the fireplace hung a painting, a landscape, not particularly good, but watching the moving flames change every second made the painting seem dead by comparison. I thought about that for a long time."

"I told him the fire would die soon," Nancy reported, "and the painting would still be there, but he just kept staring morosely at them. Perhaps the rain got him down."

Bernard took them to his favorite Italian restaurant where the lasagna was not made in February and then defrosted and microwaved in April; nothing was on the menu unless it was freshly made. Bernard, who had eaten out most of his life wherever he had lived, soon singled out restaurants worth going to and returned to them frequently enough so the waiters knew him, recommended some special dish for the day, and served him quickly. Men eating alone usually get served quickly; smart waiters know that even when they read, they don't enjoy lingering over every bite but want to fill their stomachs and get on with their day. But when Bernard brought someone to his little bistro, the waiter always let him take his time, and when it was George and Nancy he knew it would be a long evening.

They had another drink before looking at the menu, and George, who was about ten years older than Bernard, announced in a somber voice, "I did a lot of thinking while I painted those logs and looked at the landscape above them, and I made an important decision: I am going to quit teaching and just paint the rest of whatever life I may still have before me."

"You don't have to put it quite that way, George. I have

often wondered why you haven't done so before. Your paintings are selling well these days, and they are fetching high
prices. Why did you wait so long?"

"He likes to have all those young things around him,"
Nancy chipped in.

"I held on because it meant security," George answered,
ignoring Nancy's little comment. "As you know, I was quite
unfashionable for many years. Without my teaching job we
would have practically starved. Now they like me, but that
can change tomorrow. The art market needs something new
every few years."

"What gave you the courage suddenly to give up the security of your teaching position?" Bernard asked. "Do you think
your reputation is now firmly enough established so your
paintings will continue to sell even if some other style super-
sedes you?"

"We have a little money set aside," Nancy put in quickly,
"and a broker friend has invested it well."

"I am quitting because I am deeply tired of it all," George
went on, as though Nancy had not spoken. "I stopped to count
the years I might still have and decided to devote them only
to what matters. Many of those painting students don't have
any talent. They don't even want to paint. They just enjoy
being 'painters,' and sitting in outdoor cafés wearing funky
clothes, and having the tourists point at them: "Look, there's
an artist!'"

"If you do give up your teaching post, will you stay in this
area or move away?"

"I'd love to go to New Mexico," said Nancy.

"I know that, Nancy." It was the first time George had
reacted to something his wife had said. "But I'd rather stay
here. I am not looking for new scenes to paint. I want to deep-

en and make better what I do now."

Bernard looked at them, the proverbial happy couple, married for God knows how many years. How can George stand it, the way she answers for him, the way she barely lets him finish a sentence or a thought? Yet George did not seem to mind; he never interrupted her, just patiently waited for her to finish and then continued what he was saying. Looking at them, Bernard felt good about living alone.

"Here I've been talking about myself all the time," George went on, "and I haven't even asked you what's new in your life."

"Nothing much. I have a new student."

"That's hardly news."

"It is in this case."

"How so?" Nancy raised her head from the menu.

"Is he exceptionally talented?" George wanted to know.

"It's a she and she is talented, but that's not all."

"Is she very pretty?" Nancy was looking at him.

"Yes, she is attractive, but that's not what makes her different either."

"Well, what is it then?"

"I really don't know yet, George, but all my life I've known the first time I met someone new whether he or she would be important to me."

"Is it something sexual?" Nancy asked.

"In the widest use of the term, all encounters between men and women are sexual. Mitzi once told me that a woman knows the moment she lays eyes on a man, whether she will go to bed with him or not, if he asks her. I remember telling her that men are aware of that and read it in a woman's eyes."

"Oh, come on," George said. "These things develop

slowly and grow—"

"I know what he means"—Nancy was on his side for once—"but you haven't told us much about the young lady."

"What would you like to know?"

"First of all, what does she look like?"

"Well, she is tall, actually a little taller than I am. Her hair is light blond—natural, I think—her eyes a clear blue. Her face is lean and well-shaped . . . she is altogether well-shaped."

"Sounds good. Does she remind you of Mitzi?"

"No, not at all. What really impressed me is her profound love of music, undiluted by vanity or ambition, her sensitivity to the varieties of sound, and her truly extraordinary musical memory. During the years of her marriage—she is divorced now—she did not play the piano at all, and yet she remembers all the music she has ever learned. Quite a feat, I think."

"You need a new friend in your life." George rejoined their conversation. "You have lived alone too long. Perhaps you should get married again. To have someone to take care of you and look after you when you are down in the world, someone to stand beside you when things go well, someone to share your ups and downs with you."

"I like your definition of a good companion, but I am not actively looking. These things happen only when you are *not* looking for them; I am firmly convinced of that."

"Perhaps you are right. But one has to be open to new possibilities, new encounters, new experiences."

"Especially sexual ones?" goaded Nancy.

"Not more than others," George continued. He turned to Bernard. "Have you ever thought of quitting your teaching?"

"Absolutely not. When you teach piano privately there is no such thing as retirement. Luckily I am not a boxer or a ballerina. Their professional lives are short. I can continue teaching till I drop dead. My own teacher, that grand old Russian lady—you met her once—taught until she was ninety-five. Kept her alive, she always said."

"Don't you see yourself playing golf somewhere in eternal sunshine?" Nancy asked.

Bernard looked at her closely. She must have been stunningly beautiful when she was young. She still looked good; her features had sharpened somewhat with age, but they had not deteriorated. He wondered whether George still saw the young girl when he looked at her. She helped George in many ways, kept their finances in order, paid their bills, kept unwelcome visitors out of his studio, and maintained social contact with people she thought might advance his career. She could be most charming with potential buyers of George's paintings. But for Bernard she was too mundane, too obsessed with trivia. He had an image of her finding George in a genuine depression and offering him food, forcing him to eat it while saying, "But it's good for you." Bernard would not have liked to have her around when he was in such a mood.

Bernard had a very intense dream about his mother that night. Had Nancy brought memories of his mother back into his subconscious? Not likely, the two were so different from each other. In his dream his mother had entered his room, as she had often done in real life, in the middle of the night when she had woken him to make him part of one of her fantasies. He had taken on many roles in those nightly encounters; he had to go with her wherever her mind chose to dwell. Once she talked to him as though he were her own father and had pleaded with him not to strike her.

"I won't do it again, I promise. Please don't hit me, I

promise I'll never do it again."

He had tried to get through to her. "I'm your son. I'm Bernard."

"You're just saying that."

Another time he had been the Gestapo officer who had come to arrest his father. She had stood in the doorway, trying to prevent him from entering.

"You can't take my husband away. He hasn't done anything. I won't let you, do you hear? I just won't let you."

In his dream that night she had come carrying a long kitchen knife. She had come with the intention of killing him, as she had once come in real life. If his poor bewildered father had not woken up and stopped her, she might have done it. His father had subdued her, and the next morning Bernard heard telephone conversations about her being put away. He had never been so frightened again in all his life. During his adolescence she had been a regular partner in his nightmares. He had also been afraid of becoming like her unless he kept tight control over his own brain and never let it slip into fantasies. Once he had even tried to convince her that if she kept control over her brain, she would be well again.

"But I *am* well," she had answered, with her most disarming smile. In those calm, quiet moments one forgot how terrible she could be when carried away by some wild flight of her imagination. As a boy Bernard had often been angry with her for being what she was. Why did he have to have such a mother when all the other boys had normal ones?

Chapter 5

LYDIA MADE RAPID PROGRESS, AND THE DAMAGE DONE BY eight years of neglect was repaired in a few weeks. She played as well as ever again. After her sixth lesson she remained sitting at the keyboard when Bernard got up from his chair next to her to indicate that the lesson was over.

"Mr. Winter," she said, looking down at the keys.

"Yes?"

"Mr. Winter, you have these two lovely grand pianos right next to each other. Could we ever play two-piano music together?"

He leaned over the back of the piano and faced her light hair. "Have you played on two pianos before?"

She looked up at him with that smile he had begun to recognize. "No, but I think it must be lots of fun."

"It is." He hesitated for a moment. "I'll tell you what: Let's play together on two pianos, by all means. But not as part of your lesson. Let us do it just for our own pleasure."

"I was hoping you would say something like that."

"Perhaps I have not said it clearly enough. What I mean is that when we play on two pianos we shall do so as equals and I won't take any money from you for my time." What an awkward way of putting it! "It would be like a therapist who sleeps with one of his female patients charging her for those sessions," he added, before he realized how it would sound.

Lydia gave him a look of bewilderment. Her smile had disappeared, but she said nothing.

"I'll tell you what," he continued. I'm even repeating myself like a retarded child! "What I mean is that we should meet at a time when I don't teach, perhaps on the weekend. " Control, control! "I am free on Saturdays and Sundays. How would you like to come here next Saturday afternoon? We'll play some music on two pianos and then go out for dinner. How does that sound to you?"

"I'd like that very much."

Quite the teacher again, he went to a corner of his studio and took some music off the lowest shelf.

"Music I use rarely I keep on the lower shelves. This is my two-piano corner. Actually, there isn't that much really first-class music for this idiom. Mozart wrote only one sonata for two pianos—quite a few for one piano, four hands—and there are the Brahms Haydn-Variations, of course, and we'll try this *Petite suite* by Borodin. It is quite charming."

There were two copies of all the pieces he had taken off the shelf. He separated them and handed Lydia one of each. "Do take this music home with you and look it over between now and Saturday."

"Of course I will! I can't wait to get it into my fingers. Which part shall I take, first piano or second?"

"First, of course." With a gentle European bow from the hips.

"That doesn't seem right, somehow."

"In music that is idiomatically written for two pianos, such as the pieces you are taking with you, the two parts are truly equal. It is not that the second piano serves as an accompaniment to the first. There is a constant give-and-take—all ensemble music has that element—a little like a marriage or a longtime liaison." *What is the matter with me today?* "But if it troubles you in any way, please take the second part in the Brahms. It'll make for more variety."

"Good. That makes me feel better, Mr. Winter." *I wish she'd stop calling me that!* "I can see there's a lot more music on those lower shelves. What else is down there?"

"Some of it is for one piano, four hands. I've had it since I was a teenager. I also have some pieces arranged for two pianos. I now prefer original compositions, but I have kept them."

"Kept them? What do you mean?"

"I find it difficult to throw printed music into the garbage, no matter how bad it is."

"Oh. May I look at it some day?"

"If you like."

"So you have done some two-piano playing?"

"Yes, many years ago in Rome."

"I didn't know you lived in Rome."

"As a student I had my year there."

"That must have been wonderful. Did you like it?"

"I loved it. I asked them to renew my scholarship, but they didn't, and I had to come home when I ran out of money."

"Was your two-piano partner a man or a woman?"

"A man, a fellow student. We actually contemplated making a career as a duo-piano team, but it came to nothing when I had to go home."

On his way back from Rome to New York, Bernard had stopped in Vienna, where Mitzi was doing several roles at the Volksoper, though not yet at the Staatsoper. He wanted to see her, perhaps to clear things up between them by talking about them. He anticipated their first encounter after that mutual disclosure of infidelities with some apprehension; knowing the volatility of her temper, he had no idea how she would receive him. When he arrived at her pension, a solid establishment in the central part of Vienna, she embraced him with genuine affection. When they entered her room, which was well furnished, if not overly elegant, he was aware of the contrast to his dingy New York apartment, trying to converse above the noise of the subway or ignoring it by making love or music.

Mitzi led the way to two heavily ornamented armchairs. They sat down and talked for a while about trivial matters. There was no mention of recent events in their lives or the exchange of letters dealing with them.

Although Mitzi had been in several German-speaking cities, her German was still rudimentary and she wanted to show off her American husband, who spoke it so fluently.

"Let's go downstairs," she suggested.

"By all means."

She introduced him to the owner of the pension, a buxom lady with golden braids, and to the porter, and he gained their friendship quickly by chatting with them in their own tongue. When he spoke to his wife and called her Mitzi in front of the porter, she quickly pulled him by the sleeve and whispered in his ear, "I don't use that name anymore."

The porter strained his ear—he surely knew no English—and she pulled him even farther away.

"I've been told that the Austrian upper class never uses Mitzi as a diminutive for Margaret," she explained, "so I've changed my name to Gretel. Gretel Winter, very Viennese."

He had to suppress a laugh. "All right, Mitzi," he said, "I'll call you Gretel while I'm here."

As a music student, Bernard was anxious to see Vienna; there are not many towns in Europe with such a concentration of musical activity and talent. He asked her to take him to all the places he had read about: Schubert's birthplace; Heiligenstadt, where Beethoven supposedly wrote his "Heiligenstadt Testament;" and various other places associated with Haydn, Mozart, Brahms, and Strauss. She had not been to any of them.

"I came to Vienna to sing," she said, "not to act like a tourist."

"Mitzi—Gretel, I mean—how can you live in this town and not want to see those places?"

"I sing mostly Verdi and Puccini," came the reply, "and they have nothing to do with this town."

She did take him to the Spanische Reitschule and together they admired the trained horses. She also took him to some fine restaurants; to the *Heurigen* in Grinzing, where they had a little too much of a slightly sour wine; and to her favorite café, where she was clearly known and respected and where the waiter immediately put a tray full of pastries before her. She took her time choosing one and gave Bernard a running commentary on the merits of each of them as she pointed at them with her finger.

The Music Teacher

They had what is considered a good time but, as Bernard sensed, the flame was not burning as fiercely in him as before. She noticed it too. "Have those lousy Italians eaten the marrow out of your bones?" she asked him one night when he could not muster the passion for a third act of congress. "I'm just a little tired," he had said, but he also saw it as a symbol.

"At the end of the summer, after the *Festspiele* are over, I'll be back in New York; then we can have a proper marriage again," Margaret-Mitzi-Gretel consoled him.

But she did not come back in the fall. She had received a number of guest engagements, as she explained in her letter, and turning them down would be tantamount to not being available, and if you are not around, she concluded, you are quickly forgotten.

That was certainly true, as Bernard found out when he returned to New York. All his fellow students had either taken jobs in other towns, gotten married, or just disappeared. His former teacher inquired politely into the details of Bernard's study in Rome but had to dismiss him when a student appeared for his lesson. He went to the placement office of his former school to find out what sort of work he could find to support himself. A kindly older woman asked what he had in mind, and he answered truthfully that he didn't know. As long as it is in New York, he added. There are very few of those to be had, he was told. He drafted a letter to his Uncle Willie, saying that he needed further study and would like to do postgraduate work. He tore it up when he imagined Uncle Willie reading it. How long, Uncle Willie would say, can you remain a student?

The next few days he spent in his cheap hotel room doing absolutely nothing but staring at the dirty spots on the ceiling above his bed. That must have been what my mother did for days on end. I must get out of this; I need to make music, to play the piano. He put a volume of Beethoven sonatas into his briefcase, went to his former school, and opened practice room doors until he found an empty one. It had only an upright piano and not a very good one at that, but it was all he needed. He played one sonata after another, as they came chronologically in the volume, singing the melodies and stamping his foot on the pedal, and felt the blood in his veins again. He played until he heard the familiar bell ring in the hallways, which meant it was ten minutes to ten and the building would be closed shortly.

As he left the practice room reluctantly, one of the janitors recognized him. "Haven't seen you in a while. You still a student here?"

"Yes. I've just been away for a year." The man did not have to know everything.

The following morning he went back to the placement office where the same kindly woman was on duty.

"Well," she said with a friendly smile, "so you're back. Have you decided what kind of work you would like to do?"

"Yes, I want something that involves playing the piano."

"That would mean accompanying lessons. Do you have a preference?"

He looked at her uncomprehendingly.

"Would you like to accompany voice, instrumental, or dance lessons?"

"Dance," he said quickly. It might be fun to watch pretty young female bodies as they went through various positions and contortions.

"Modern or ballet?"

"Makes no difference," he said in his ignorance.

"Let me see. One of the ballet classes needs an accompanist. They meet from nine to eleven every morning in studio D. That's on the fourth floor, next to the large rehearsal hall. Shall I put your name down?"

"Please do."

Watching the young bodies move turned out to be less entertaining than he had thought, and playing incessantly for two full hours was quite a strain. Bernard did not know how to improvise and thus had to draw on his memory to fill those two hours with sounds. The instructor, a wiry young woman with muscular legs and a flat chest, often complained about his choice of music.

"Play something more rhythmic, she would say, "and less complicated, please."

Bach fugues were obviously not the proper thing for the occasion; neither was late Beethoven or anything that sounded like Schoenberg. Chopin mazurkas, on the other hand, were appreciated and the class did not mind having them repeated. In fact, they liked it. Repeating the music made the two hours pass more quickly.

After class Bernard waited for the girls to dress and went to lunch with them. They tolerated his presence but showed no interest in anything except their own bodies. They talked about injuries they had sustained, movements they found difficult or painful, and what tired them. They did not miss Bernard when he stopped going to lunch with them.

Slightly embarrassed but determined, Bernard went back to the placement bureau. "Do you have any openings in the instrumental department?"

"What's wrong with dance?"

"Nothing wrong. I just thought playing with a violinist or a cellist might be musically more interesting."

"Let me see what there is."

"You have been very patient with me," Bernard added.

She took off her glasses and looked at him with gray eyes. "That is part of my job. And you seem in particular need of our help. Yes, there is something. You're quite lucky. One of our best violin teachers has asked for a new pianist. The girl who played for him is getting married."

Bernard, who had avoided playing for voice lessons because it would have reminded him too much of his first year with Mitzi —he never thought of her as Gretel—showed up the next morning at the violin teacher's studio, hoping to get to play some real pieces. He soon found out, to his chagrin, that the famous teacher worked mostly on different positions of the hand and arm, on bowings and fingerings. The students played Paganini, Wieniawski, Vieuxtemps, and other typical composers of violin music. The Brahms sonatas Bernard had hoped to get acquainted with in these lessons were apparently studied in chamber music classes. It was better, though, than playing for the ballet students. Here there were long breaks when the teacher talked, explained, and demonstrated, and Bernard did not have to improvise, for which he had neither talent nor liking.

He now earned enough money to rent a room with a piano. Near the music school, many such rooms were available. He no longer had to open doors of practice rooms and live in fear of being caught by the janitor. He spent his afternoons practicing a recital program which he saw no possibility of ever giving. He worked at it studiously, though, and changed repertoire occasionally to bring it nearer to what he considered perfection.

Then came a letter from Margaret:

The Music Teacher

My dear Bernard,

I don't think I'll be coming back to New York in the foreseeable future, and at the moment I don't have the money to send you a ticket for a visit here. I would rather have told you this in person than in a letter: There is a man here who wants to marry me. He is a banker, enormously wealthy. I would never again have to worry about money, as long as I live. You do understand, don't you? And, after all, our marriage was never really a success. You'll have to agree with me there. Please make the necessary legal arrangements.

Bernard did not leave his room for almost two weeks. He called the violin teacher to report sick, and heated canned spaghetti on an electric plate whenever he was hungry. Lying on his bed, he watched the black spots and the peeling plaster designs on the ceiling. They took on many shapes, most of them abstract figurations, but occasionally they looked a little like Margaret. There was a metal grating on his window to prevent burglars from entering—what would they steal, his piano?—and he counted its parts many times, up and down. He saw no reason to go on living, to stay in this room forever and accompany violin lessons, but he lacked the energy and the courage to do anything drastic.

Near the end of the second week the violin teacher called to ask whether Bernard was getting better. He told him in a faint voice that he was never coming back to play for his students, and half an hour later there was a loud knock at his door. It was the violin teacher, a small man with sleek black hair, perhaps too flawlessly black for a man his age.

"You sounded a little strange on the telephone," he said.

"I thought I'd better look in on you. Are you all right?"

He sat down in Bernard's only chair and began to talk about how the young give up hope too easily and how small disappointments seem enormous to them. He went on with greater emphasis to say why it was better to live *with* music, on *any* level, than not to live at all. He had been in touch with the young all his life and thought he understood them.

At first Bernard resented this intrusion in his private grief, but slowly he began to respect the little man, even to like him. How wrong I was to think of him as a mechanic of the violin, only interested in fingerings and bowings.

"Get dressed," the man was saying. "Get dressed and we'll go out and eat something together."

He took Bernard to a modest but excellent restaurant, and afterward they went to the concert of a famous violinist whom Bernard had never heard. When the virtuoso came on stage it seemed as though a ray of sunshine had come with him, he exuded such a happy conviction of his own excellence. Is that what you need to succeed? Bernard asked himself.

His savior was reading the program notes. "He gave his first recital at age eleven," he quoted.

Perhaps you need to encounter success early in life to really believe in it. Too late for me, Bernard thought.

As though he were reading his thoughts, the violin teacher turned to Bernard and said, "But you know, other people begin their careers when they are in their forties. It is really *never* too late, if you continue to grow and develop."

This funny old man with his bowings and fingerings had helped him to return to active life. Bernard often remembered him and those days of despair. Thoughts of suicide do come more often to the young. Perhaps, as we encounter misfortune later in life, we understand that a single event is not reason enough to give up everything, though we are often tempted to think so at any age.

Would anything that could happen to me today affect me similarly? he wondered. Does Lydia ever have serious depressions and what would cause them? Probably nothing as desperate as the catatonic state his mother often fell into in the early stages of her illness. Would he ever know Lydia well enough to touch such a topic with her, even on a conversational level, if not a personal one?

I need to get closer to her, closer in every way, he thought. Sometimes when I bend over her to demonstrate something on the piano and accidentally touch her, I feel something akin to what happened to me when I first met Mitzi. Should a man my age still have such feelings?

The morning after the violin teacher had taken him to the concert, Bernard was back at the placement office. "You must be thoroughly sick of me," he said as he entered.

"No, I'm not," said the ever-helpful lady, "and if I may inject a personal comment, I think you are in need of a real change in your life. You don't mind my saying that?"

"Not at all. What would you suggest?"

"I have a request from a large midwestern university for an assistant professor to teach piano and chamber music. Would you consider that?"

"In my present mood I would indeed."

"Even if it included teaching a class in music appreciation?"

"Why not? I have never done that. It would be something new for me."

$$Chapter\ 6$$

THE SHEER SIZE OF THE MIDWESTERN UNIVERSITY OVER-
whelmed Bernard when he arrived there, with its well-kept
lawns, old trees, and red brick buildings connected by paved
walkways. Quite different from litter-strewn Central Park on
a Sunday afternoon.

The students walking about flaunting their blond hair and
pink flesh also astonished him. To a young man who had
grown up in the Washington Heights section of New York and
knew only Paris and Rome on the other side of the ocean,
they all looked like brothers and sisters.

Even around the music building, named after a rich
donor, the boys and girls carrying cello and trombone cases
were blond and pink. So they weren't all physical education
majors, as he had first thought. At his New York school the
majority of his fellow students had been dark and looked
slightly sickly, at least by comparison to these youngsters.
When Bernard opened the doors to a band rehearsal room he
saw rows and rows of shiny trumpets and horns, not to men-

tion innumerable flutes and clarinets. No wonder midwestern bands had such a rich sound.

He, who had spent the preceding years largely alone with his piano, was suddenly asked to attend a large number of faculty meetings and social events, within his department and college-wide. Often the topics of discussion at the formal meetings appeared trivial to him, but he was impressed by the vigor, the stubborn bitterness, and animosity that some of his colleagues displayed. At social gatherings these feuds were hidden or temporarily buried, and Bernard enjoyed listening to conversations between mathematicians, physicists, and others engaged in fields he knew little about.

His living quarters were plain but pleasant, on the second floor of a Victorian building that had been divided up into small apartments. It was situated on a residential street within walking distance of the college; from his window he actually saw a row of juniper bushes under an old oak tree, quite a change from the airshaft in his parents' apartment. But, best of all, in his studio in the music building there were two Steinway grands just for his use. What luxury!

His piano students were only a few years younger than he, and he enjoyed working with them. Their love of music was as great as any he had encountered in his own school, but they were much less competitive and jealous of one another. He knew how to deal with them. What puzzled him was the music appreciation class he had also agreed to teach. It took place in a large classroom, complete with record and tape player, a grand piano, and visual aids equipment.

The textbook he had been handed seemed misguided to him. Why should all these potential engineers and accountants know the plots of operas they would probably never see? Why should they memorize a number of Italian, French, and

German expressions that would have no meaning for them later—except to shine at cocktail parties—and why should they learn details of the often boring lives of those who had composed music?

Bernard, who had associated mostly with people whose entire lives were devoted to music—ever since his friendship with Peter—had no idea what music meant to the rest of the world. He was in for a shock.

He decided to spend the first session of his music appreciation class playing a simple Schubert piece for his students and then asking them to tell him what they had heard. At first no one spoke at all. Shyness, he thought. Then a little girl in the first row did speak up. It sounded like a country scene, she said, with a little mist on it. Did she notice how the main melody came back near the end? Silence.

"What main melody?" a husky fellow asked.

These were not music students, after all. One hearing was not enough for them.

"I'll play it again," he told them. "This time listen carefully and tell me whether the main melody, the one I begin with, comes back exactly the same way when it appears again near the end of the piece, or whether it is in any way different."

He looked around the room when he finished playing. Not a single hand was raised. I'll have to be even more obvious, he thought, as he went back to the piano. This time he just played the opening tune, a typical happy Schubertian melody, and repeated it immediately in the minor mode, as Schubert might have done.

"Did you hear any difference between these two versions?" he asked.

Another long silence. What am I doing wrong? Why don't they respond? What is the matter here?

The Music Teacher

"It sounded as though the tune had turned sour the second time around," a big blond boy volunteered.

"Thank God you *do* hear something."

When he discussed this with Professor Saunders, an older colleague who also taught music appreciation, Saunders said, "Our kind of music means nothing to these kids. They are barely able to recognize the pop tunes they hear thousands of times every day—their radios are always on—and they haven't the faintest idea that music can be more than an ever-present background to their conversations and studies. They are totally unaware of music's deeper meaning or emotional impact."

"What do we teach them then?"

"Just make them read what's in the textbook," Saunders advised, "and give them a stiff exam at the end of the term. They want grades, not information. I use a multiple-choice exam myself—I just change a few questions every year—so I don't have to decipher their handwriting. I leave *that* to the English professors."

Bernard was not yet willing to give up. In the next class he played another short piece for them, Schumann this time, and asked them to write their thoughts on a piece of paper—anything that occurred to them—from a paragraph to a page. That evening he read sixty-five "reviews" of the Schumann piece. Almost all of them found it pretty, the most widely used adjective. Some compared it to a popular song he did not know, and others wrote a movie scenario to go along with it.

I must try different approaches, he concluded. Surely this is my fault. I have not thought this through properly. Perhaps I should discuss it with some of the younger teachers. When he did, he found out that they all followed the textbook, not because they believed in it but because Professor Saunders was on the tenure committee, and there was no point in antagonizing him.

At the next departmental meeting Bernard asked to speak.

"I think we need to reconsider our music appreciation program," he began. "It seems to me that we give our students a great deal of information, but we don't teach them anything about the language of music and its meaning."

There was total silence in the room. The older members of the faculty stared at Bernard, and the younger ones looked at the chairman to await his response. When there was none, Bernard continued. "Perhaps each instructor should be given greater freedom in the choice of a textbook as well as in his general approach."

The chairman waited again. When Bernard sat down, he said, "You need to know, Professor Winter, that our present textbook was selected by a departmental committee that functioned for two years before making its choice. Then the entire department voted for its adoption. The book remains in use until a new committee is formed, perhaps three years from now, to review the matter. When the time comes I will keep in mind that you have expressed a desire to be on that committee. I cannot guarantee, of course, that you will be."

Professor Saunders, three chairs down from on Bernard's left, had a broad grin on his face.

At the president's reception for new faculty members, Bernard noticed a tall woman with caramel-colored hair and an athletic figure. She moved about the room freely, speaking to people here and there. He was hoping she would come his way, and after a while she did.

"I'm Philippa Howland," she said, "Dean Howland's wife."

"My name is Winter, Bernard Winter."

"Glad to meet you. And what is your department, Mr. Winter?"

"Music."

"Are you a musicologist or a composer?"

"Neither. I'm a pianist."

"Oh, how nice! I love the piano; actually, it is my favorite instrument. I can listen to it forever. Will you play for us?"

"What do you mean? Right here? Now?"

"No, of course not. I meant for the college community, sometime this winter. What I really love is to hear someone practice. When I listen to a pianist go over certain spots many times, I feel I'm really getting to know the music. Do you mind having someone in the room when you practice, Mr. Winter?"

"Not at all," he lied. Not if she is the dean's wife, he had almost said.

"When do you usually practice?"

"Oh, around five, after classes are over."

"Well, you might hear a little knock on your studio door one of these afternoons."

She turned and left to speak to someone else. Professor Saunders, who had been standing nearby, came over with a warning. "Beware of Dean Howland's wife. She eats young men for breakfast."

"She's a lovely woman," was all that came to Bernard's mind.

A few days later, as he was trying to get the third variation of the arietta in Beethoven's Opus 111 sonata right—he had struggled with it for years—there was a discreet knock on his door. It was Philippa, in tennis shorts and sneakers.

"Please don't stop. I'll just sit quietly in that chair in the corner."

He continued to work on the third variation—though not without some self-conscious unease—and when he looked in the direction of her chair, about an hour later, she was gone.

The following day she knocked again, at exactly five minutes past five, he happened to notice. This time she wore a skirt and a blouse. Bernard was working on Schumann's *Carnaval*, and when he came to the piece called "Chopin" she was standing behind him, her breasts touching his shoulders lightly.

"I just had to know who wrote this," she said apologetically.

He turned around on his piano stool without getting up, his legs slightly apart. "It is Schumann's homage to Chopin," he explained. "He must have wanted it to sound like Chopin, but it is still very much Schumann."

She moved an inch forward between his thighs.

"It is certainly very beautiful."

"I like to play it."

"And you play it awfully well."

She stepped back to the window. Bernard kept a bottle of Scotch whisky in the closet between the bust of Beethoven, which was too heavy to be moved, and the photographs his predecessor had left hanging on the studio walls. Should he offer her some? She accepted, and they sat down next to each other on the sofa, slowly sipping their drinks and looking at each other.

I still had all my hair then, Bernard thought, and I was a lot slimmer than I am now. His hand went to her hair, and he began to stroke it gently. She laughed softly and continued to look at him. He unfastened her blouse and reached under it.

Her whole body stretched toward him. Her skirt came off easily and seconds later he was inside her as the light faded slowly through the window. There was an awkward moment when her head hit the armrest of the sofa as he pulled her down, but she just laughed.

When they were back in a sitting position, she said, "I knew that you liked women the moment I saw you."

"Don't most men?"

"Not quite that way. Some men use women to enhance their own image; some enjoy humiliating us; others put their heads between our breasts and think they're back with Mama. But you . . . you truly like women for what they are."

He kissed her.

"And that," she added, "is why women are attracted to you."

He was ready to start all over. "No, my dear Bernard." She pushed him back. "No more this afternoon."

She got up, dressed quickly, and said, in the tone of voice he had heard at the cocktail party, "I *am* the dean's wife and I intend to remain that. I'd love to see you again, Bernard, but it will have to be handled very discreetly. Absolutely no one must know about us, students or faculty, least of all the dean. It is not easy to keep a secret in a university town. Do you think you can carry it off?"

This appealed to Bernard's sense of adventure. It also suited him to meet a woman without emotional complications on her part, without obligations on his, a woman older and more experienced than he.

He worked out a careful plan for their illicit meetings. There was a large motel near the airport and since she, as the dean's wife, often had to take visitors to and from the airport, the presence of her white convertible would not be noticed at the airport's parking lot. On Wednesday afternoon, the day they always met, Bernard would register at the airport motel—if you paid the so-called day rate you did not have to identify yourself; you just had to be out by 4 P.M.—then sit in the coffee shop until she arrived. She would walk past his table and say hello while he told her the room number. A few minutes later they would both be in the room, their clothes off, and in bed.

One day, after they had known each other for a while, she said, "I knew it would be good with you." Then, looking at herself, she went on. "My body is really all I've got, and I like to use it. I have no talents whatsoever; if I stop being the dean's wife, I'll just be nothing."

She did know how to use her body and initiated Bernard into many variants of the sexual act. The possibilities seemed limited only by her imagination and taste. Whereas sex had been the fulfillment of a deep need to Mitzi, it was just a joyful activity to Philippa. She often laughed in the middle of things, which Bernard preferred to the sighing and moaning of others. In some ways she was my most satisfying lover, he thought, years later.

Among his students were two girls who liked to linger after their lesson, but Bernard did not encourage them. "It's considered all right, as long as they are graduate students," Saunders had once told him, but Bernard, young as he was, felt fatherly toward his students and made it a principle never to get involved, emotionally or physically.

With the exception of one dismal lapse—a girl who had literally thrown herself at him and threatened suicide if he rejected her—he had remained loyal to this principle until the appearance of Lydia. Whenever he had been tempted, he had squelched the urge before it had had a chance to develop. Why was it different with Lydia? Had he reached a dangerous age, as popular books and newspaper articles told him? Had he lived alone too long, as George thought? During their Saturday afternoon sessions, when he and Lydia played on two pianos, she was—at least technically, he rationalized— not his student, and perhaps that allowed him to break the self-imposed barrier.

Their first session on two pianos proved to be an unqual- ified success. Lydia's playing was sensitive, flexible, and of genuine ensemble quality. Whenever he speeded up or slowed down the slightest bit, she was there with him. Whenever he had the leading part, she subsided and followed him. When her part was the more important one, she rose in dynamics and led the ensemble. Bernard was very pleased and told her so. She blushed and said she had not been so happy in a long while.

The dinner was less of a success. Lydia spoke mostly about Carl: his difficulties in school, his strange and unpre- dictable behavior at home, particularly when he came back from his biweekly visits with his father. Bernard, old enough to know when to be quiet and just listen, asked only a ques- tion here and there. He wanted to hear more about her than about the boy, but he understood that he would have to wait a little before he could get nearer to her.

When they returned to his apartment building, where Lydia had left her car, she said, "Carl spends next Saturday with his father. I'd like us to go to my place after we play. I'll cook. Don't worry, I promise I won't start peeling the carrots after you arrive. It'll all be ready when we get there."

Bernard was pleased by the offer, although he was by no means sure whether it should be perceived as a symbol of their new equality or a promise of intimacy.

Chapter 7

NEAR THE END OF HIS SECOND YEAR AT THE MIDWESTERN
university, Bernard had had a letter from Israel. It was from
his old friend Ronit, the girl who had been near him when he
lost a competition and when he won one. She wrote that she
had become assistant to the head of a music conservatory in
Jerusalem. Her school was running a summer course for
pianists with the accent on repertoire. They were inviting
experts in a number of fields. Would he be interested in
teaching a course on modern American piano music? They
would pay for his trip, make an apartment in Jerusalem available to him, and there would be a small honorarium. At the
bottom of the letter Ronit added in her hardly legible handwriting that she had gotten married and was the mother of a
girl named Liora.

The letter jolted Bernard out of the routine life into
which he had bogged down. Israel, my oh my! He had not
paid much attention to political developments in the world

and even less to his Jewishness. He was aware of it, would never deny it, if asked, but it had little concrete meaning for him. He had often been told that he did not look Jewish, with his wavy brown hair, deep-set blue eyes, straight nose, and square chin. He probably looked more German than anything else.

His father had gone to synagogue on the High Holidays and had taken young Bernard with him. The images Bernard retained from those visits were rows and rows of men with prayer shawls around their shoulders bending forward and back with a swaying motion while mumbling in semiunison, occasionally shouting out a word in full voice; individuals being called up to the Torah—an honor his father never enjoyed—which was then read off at a speed no one could possibly understand; and long sermons by a sweaty man who liked to raise his arm and point his forefinger at the congregation when he thought they were not paying enough attention.

There was one positive exception to those childhood memories of religious service: An East European cantor—German Jews looked down on East Europeans as primitive, uneducated people who had not produced a Heine or an Einstein—a "hazan," as it was called, had visited Bernard's hometown. His reputation was so great that the entire Jewish community came to hear him pray, and Bernard was allowed to go with his father to the evening service. Hershel *der meshuggener* (the crazy one), as the disapproving majority called him, was a short, hefty man who sang with the rare voice of a dramatic tenor and added melismas and coloraturas to the traditional tunes of the prayers As the evening wore on he reached a state that can only be described as religious ecstasy. He swayed, but with conviction, and had almost operatic sequences to his singing. The combination of religious fervor and musical invention—he did make up all those coloratura passages—made a deep and lasting impression on Bernard. His father thought the man had gone too far, as he explained to Bernard on the way home.

Bernard's father had kept the Jewish tradition of saying the Kaddish, the prayer for the dead, on the anniversary of the day his own father had died. Bernard was somehow in awe of that prayer. He remembered the opening words: *Yisgadal veyiskadash*. He had been told that in the extermination camps people spoke those words as they went to their own death. Before succumbing to the injuries inflicted on his body in the Dachau concentration camp, Bernard's father had given him a small prayer book and asked him to say Kaddish every year on the anniversary of his death—the date to be determined by the Jewish calendar. Since he had died on Yom Kippur—only saintly people were fortunate enough to die on such a sacred day—it was easy to remember. Whenever Bernard found out the date for Yom Kippur—it was even announced in *The New York Times*—he got out his little prayer book and said Kaddish, but always in the privacy of his room. He never went to a synagogue to say Kaddish in the midst of a group of swaying men.

To Bernard the establishment of the state of Israel was the only logical reply to what Hitler's legions had done to the Jews of Europe, and he was proud of the military prowess the young people there had displayed. He had read they were arrogant and looked down upon the survivors of the Holocaust who had, as they saw it, let themselves be slaughtered without defending themselves. He was curious to see these strong young people and to meet them. Yes, he would accept Ronit's invitation. He wrote to her immediately.

The course in Jerusalem was scheduled to run for six weeks, and he had three months of summer vacation. He decided to spend the whole summer traveling and booked passage on a Dutch ship—reputed to be well run—for the Atlantic crossing and on an Italian one—better than Greek—for the Genoa-to-Haifa stretch. He would cross Europe slowly by train with stops here and there. The voyage took much longer in those days, Bernard reminisced, but how much more pleasant it was! Walking on deck, watching the water go past at different ends of the ship, looking at the stars at night, flirting a little, and eating well. How much better than to be squeezed into the narrow seats of an airplane with three hundred ill-tempered tourists, to face all the airport annoyances and the plastic food. Those days at sea also gave you a chance to disconnect yourself from what you were used to and prepare yourself for what lay ahead. It was like a desirable neutral territory in between, a little world in itself.

Bernard did not know what to expect on his arrival in Jerusalem. On his first day there Ronit took him to the Yad Vashem Museum. There he saw for the first time photos of concentration camps and their emaciated inmates. Ronit saw on his face how upset he was.

"My father was in Dachau, you know. Long before there were extermination camps. He got out before the war because one of my mother's relatives sent an affidavit of support. I was too small to remember any of it. But they beat my father so severely, one of his kidneys was totally incapacitated and the other functioned only partially. That and the two heart attacks he suffered there made him almost an invalid when we came to America. His heart was just a rag. When he asked his American doctor whether he could have an occasional cigarette, the doctor told him, 'In your case, Mr. Winter, it doesn't make any difference whether you do or don't.' Father woke up one morning and asked for a glass of water. When I brought it to him, he was dead."

Ronit listened to him in silence and took him to a quiet monastery garden on one of the hills overlooking the old city of Jerusalem. They sat under tall poplar trees and watched the reflections of the sun on the golden dome of the Mosque of Omar. Next she took him to the Wailing Wall, or Western Wall, as it is now called. There he stood for a long time and watched men in long black coats, prayer shawls around their necks, praying and swaying while occasionally touching the stones of the wall. Here they are, he thought, in their own country, free and still enmeshed in the ancient grief. He respected the intensity of their belief, which had survived innumerable massacres, but he did not feel that he was their brother. Were the young teachers at his American university more his brothers than these men? Not either.

They stayed till sunset and then went to the conservatory, where the opening ceremony of the summer course was held in the evening. Ronit's boss spoke briefly and members of the faculty were introduced: a thin old lady from France with a pince-nez in her hand who was going to lecture on Debussy; a professorial-looking man, cruelly overdressed for a warm summer evening—the Beethoven expert; a contentious bearded young man who would discuss Israel's own composers; and Bernard, to represent America. The hall was packed.

"Do all these people play the piano?" he asked Ronit.

"Israel has more pianos per capita than any other country in the world," she whispered back.

* * *

The Music Teacher

Bernard found his students intense and demanding. They had passionate feelings and strong convictions about music. Nothing he said went unquestioned; bitter debates ensued in class between students, debates not easily settled. When he played something for them, a student might get up as soon as he finished, play the same phrase differently, and challenge him to defend his interpretation. Bernard had never known such students. His course took place in the morning, but he spent almost every afternoon with his students, singly or in groups, to continue the discussions they had begun in class. Their vitality infused him with energy and a need to formulate his own beliefs better.

In presenting modern American composers to his class, Bernard had tried to be absolutely fair and, in order to be comprehensive, had included a number of compositions in whose artistic validity he did not himself believe. The students sensed this immediately and questioned his honesty in presenting those pieces.

Not all the discussion and argument dealt with music. As time went on, they turned more and more to political and philosophical topics. The questions the students asked were direct and often very personal. While they represented a total spectrum of beliefs, as they would in any other country, they were posed without any Anglo-Saxon reticence.

"If you are a Jew—and you say your father was in a German concentration camp"—a subtle Israeli distinction, since the Russians also had concentration camps—"if you are a Jew, then why don't you come and live here?"

"What does it really mean to you, to be a Jew?"

"If all the Jews in America were to live the way you do, would there be any Jews in America two or three generations from now?"

He asked them many questions too, as openly and directly as they had asked him.

"Do you want to keep an Arab work force as sort of second-class citizens forever? Do you want to maintain an army of occupation for generations to come? Is there really no way to peace?"

Each question elicited as many responses as there were students present. Every one of them put his entire personality behind his opinion, unguardedly, unafraid. He liked them for it.

Through Ronit, word got to him that the students liked him too. He was not as authoritarian as their other teachers, older men and women who propounded ideas and tolerated no objections or deviations. Bernard was delighted and a little amazed at how quickly he had become accepted by this society. One evening Ronit's boss, the head of the conservatory, while sitting next to him at a formal dinner, said, "If you should ever consider staying on and living here, we would have a position for you. Please keep that in mind."

Ronit's younger brother had joined a right-wing movement—how surprised my father would have been at the existence of a Jewish right-wing movement, he thought—a group that established new settlements in Judea and Samaria (as they called it) in the occupied West Bank (as their enemies called it). Ronit's brother was living in one of these new places. Would Bernard consider giving a concert there one weekend? He would indeed. The concert would take place on Saturday night, after sundown, but they would drive there on Friday afternoon, before sundown, since neither driving nor making music was permitted on the Sabbath. Those right-wingers are heavily infused with the ultra-orthodox, Ronit explained.

The Music Teacher

The concert turned out to be one of the most memorable evenings of Bernard's summer, if not of his entire life. Ronit, her husband, her little daughter, and he were driven to her brother's kibbutz in a military vehicle, two soldiers holding machine guns by their sides.

The concert was held outdoors. It was a moonlit night under that clear eastern sky. The piano stood on a wooden platform, and members of the settlement sat on benches and folding chairs or on blankets on the ground. On all the hill-tops around them were little white Arab houses with their rounded tops, as they must have looked for centuries except for the television antenna each of them sprouted.

Bernard's playing was inspired that evening. How could you not play your best under these circumstances? The armed soldiers who kept walking around his audience made him aware of the acute danger they were in. The beautiful sur-roundings, the warmth of his listeners, the whole atmosphere heightened every gesture, every thought in him. He knew he had never played that well in public before.

When the concert was over and he stood before his audi-ence, bowing to them repeatedly and thanking them for their applause, he had one of those rare moments of illumination in which he saw himself and his life from outside. He drew two conclusions in that visionary instant: He would not live in Israel, much as he admired the idealism of its inhabitants. Neither would he spend the rest of his life at that midwestern university. What was it Professor Saunders had once told him? "I also wanted to be a concert pianist, but I retreated into comfortable obscurity." What a hideous term, comfort-able obscurity!

Bernard understood at that moment that only music mat-tered to him and for that he needed to live near the center of the music world. He also knew he had to try, at least try, to have a career as a concert pianist.

Fate helped him. When he returned to America he found out that his Uncle William had died and left him a small legacy. If he invested the money wisely, the lawyer told him, it could add considerably to his monthly income. But he was free to do with it as he wished.

Dear Uncle Willie. You have saved me again. You have died at just the right moment for me. Bernard decided to spend the entire legacy on giving a Carnegie Hall recital. There was enough money for him to have half a year of quiet preparation.

He enjoyed writing a letter of resignation to the chairman of the music department and even sent a pretty postcard to Professor Saunders, saying he would miss him. What he needed urgently was a place to live and work in, preferably near New York, though not in the city itself. At the Carnegie Tavern he ran into a former fellow student who told him he was moving to California. The man had an apartment in one of New York's northern suburbs and was glad to have Bernard take over his lease and buy his old Steinway grand for a very reasonable sum.

Bernard did not realize at the time that these hastily found lodgings would become his permanent residence. The apartment turned out to be perfect for him from every point of view. It was near enough to the city to enable him to attend any event with ease and far enough away to avoid unnecessary distractions, noise, and assorted dangers. The building was solidly built and well kept. Neither the landlord nor the neighbors objected to his playing the piano for many hours every day. It soon became as much of a home as he had ever known.

Chapter 8

"IF YOU HAVE NEVER STOOD ALONE ON THE STAGE OF Carnegie Hall and looked into the auditorium, you'll never know how vast it seems from that point of view. Rows and rows of seats and then rows and rows of balconies. This alone is enough to scare you, not to mention that all your savings go up into air in one evening, an evening that will determine the course of your entire future life. Can you really be your best when so much pressure is concentrated upon a single event?"

Lydia listened to him attentively. They had gone to her house, as agreed, after their playing session. She had prepared a simple tasty dinner ahead of time, as she had promised, and they were sitting at the table sipping a good cognac.

"I don't know," she replied, although the question had been quite rhetorical. "When I was a young girl I often dreamed about playing in Carnegie Hall. I wondered what it would be like. Can you talk about it?"

"I'll try, Lydia, but it's not going to be easy for me. I haven't thought about it for many years. I don't even know where to begin. To walk out on that stage with all the lights on you and the applause coming from all sides—not that there were all that many people at my debut—just to walk out on that stage is a glorious moment. You think of all the people who have walked there before; almost everyone you admire has. The hall itself is so beautiful."

"I love it too."

"I guess it's not the hall you want to hear about, but the concert. Well, then: I practiced for six solid months. Luckily I was able to do that. When I had chosen the program—if you like, I'll show you one the next time we are in my studio—I played it for my former teacher and a number of colleagues and friends whose opinions I respect. I listened to their comments and criticism and accepted what I considered true and justified."

"What did you play?"

"Oh, it was a serious, heavy program, as one of the critics pointed out. I played all my favorite pieces: a Bach suite, a late Beethoven sonata, Prokofiev, and some modern American pieces. I had a manager, a minute woman who knew everybody and everything. She arranged to have the programs printed and to have some ads in the papers, and she got my photo into the Sunday *Times* under the heading 'Debut Recitals of the Week.' She had done this so many times, to her I was just another client."

"You still haven't said anything about the concert itself, about your playing."

"That's the difficult part, Lydia. You may find this hard to believe, but I don't remember playing or how I played. This had happened to me once before during a competition at my school. I had been under severe pressure then, of a different kind. When you put all your money on one horse, or all your eggs in one basket—there must be a reason for having so many ways to describe this situation—anyway, when I finally got on that stage, after all that practicing and all the preparation, my fingers played the music but my mind wasn't there with them. It had sort of canceled itself out. I just don't remember playing."

"I wonder what that would be like. How about another brandy?"

"Yes, please."

"In the terms in which my ex-husband judged everything, would you say your debut was a success or a failure?"

"Strangely enough, it was neither. I did not break down in the middle or have only ghastly reviews, so it was not a failure. Neither did it make me famous overnight. Sometimes I wish I could argue with your ex-husband about this success-failure business. There is black and there is white, but there are also millions of shades of gray in between. There are men and there are women, but men have feminine elements in them and women masculine ones, all to varying degrees."

"What did the critics think of your concert?"

"New York had more newspapers in those days," Bernard continued, in a calmer voice. "I got reviewed in the *Times*, the *Herald-Tribune*, the *New York Post*, the *World-Telegram*, *Musical America*, and *Musical Courier*. Quite a list! These days you are lucky to get *one* review in this big city of ours. My manager had told me that if she got three decent reviews out of the concert, she could get me engagements. Well, I had at least three good lines: the *Times* admired my musicality although they were not impressed by my technique; the *Tribune* thought I had nimble fingers but lacked depth or insight. The *Post* liked my Prokofiev, but not my Beethoven—someone else saw it the other way around—and according to

the *Telegram* I should have played a more grateful program—
I suppose they meant more Chopin and Liszt—and none of
that modern stuff."

"Oh, that's so maddening!"

"Yes, very, if you take every printed word seriously. My
manager did a simple thing: She took all the good lines from
the different reviews and printed them in large type on some
glossy paper, which was mailed around to get me concert
engagements. I am sure the people who got this glossy sheet
knew that all the negative stuff had been simply omitted. But
they didn't seem to mind and I got a few engagements.
Sometimes the travel expenses were larger than the fee, but
my manager said, "At your stage of the game you can't afford
to turn anything down."

"Did the concert lead to any important decisions on your
part?"

"No, the important decision had been to *give* that recital.
Afterward things sort of fell into place by themselves."

"What does that mean?"

"Well, my recital aroused enough attention for the State
Department to send me on a tour of South America. I had
some hair-raising experiences there, like playing in a temper-
ature of 110° or playing when the electricity had failed, with
just a generator lighting up the keyboard. Some other time I'll
tell you more about that trip. I also got a few engagements to
play with orchestras, minor orchestras, and a number of people wanted to study with me, serious aspirants to a pianistic
career. That's when I chose my present mode of life: to be
near New York, to observe without being involved, to teach,
to play occasionally, but to avoid the politics and pressures of
the concert business."

"Have you given up all thoughts of a solo career?"

"Look, Lydia. You know I like to play, in public and at home. You have heard me in recital and with our local chamber orchestra. I enjoy that, but I don't think of it as a career. I am not too fond of that word altogether."

Lydia got up to put a few dishes away and filled their brandy glasses once more. They sipped in silence for a while.

"I haven't talked so much about myself in a long time," Bernard said softly. "I'm a little ashamed."

"Well, you shouldn't be. I'm glad you told me these things. Don't you want us to know each other better?"

"Oh, yes, I do. It's just that I usually ask all the questions."

"Don't I know that! Now tell me what you would like to know about me."

"Everything."

She laughed. "I'll gladly tell you everything. There isn't that much to say."

"There always is. How did you grow up, for instance?"

"I had a very sheltered childhood, nothing as dramatic as yours. I lived in the house I was born in until I went to college. My father's a doctor, a general practitioner, in a small southern town where everybody knows everybody's business as well as who everybody's ancestors were. My mother kept a spotless home."

"You had a happy childhood then?"

"No, I didn't. Does anyone have a happy childhood?"

"Your parents sound like normal, sensible people. They weren't retarded, alcoholic, or practicing sadists?"

"No, of course not; But that in itself does not guarantee a happy childhood."

"What made it unhappy?"

"Well, first of all I was their second daughter. They were hoping for a son the second time around. I don't think any

man will ever fully understand the drawbacks of being a second daughter. You sense your parents' disappointment even
when you are very small. Later it becomes an accumulation of
many real, and probably some imagined, slights. I always
thought my sister was more beautiful; she was naturally ahead
of me in everything, and when my parents finally had their
boy—they had to wait several years for him—things became
worse, not better."

"You seem to have come out of it without any serious
damage."

"No visible scars." Lydia smiled. "But that feeling of being
second, second in everything, goes right through adolescence.
It gets more acute, even. As a child you have to wear the
dresses she has outgrown; later, when she is almost grown up
and preening herself in front of the mirror to meet some silly
boy, you are still a flat-chested child with spindly legs. You
have to be in bed even before she comes home from her date.
Endless small disadvantages convince you of your own
unworthiness. Maybe some older sisters are nicer than mine
was. She really enjoyed putting me down whenever she could.
She still manages to do it."

"You are getting angry, Lydia, even now."

"I always get angry when I think of her."

"Where is she now?"

The phone rang. Lydia went to her bedroom to answer it
and came back several minutes later.

"That was Carl," she said, after sitting down again, "calling from his father's place. Apparently he was left alone; his
father had to leave on some urgent business. I don't like it one
bit but I'm afraid it's typical. As I was calming Carl down, his
father got back. Otherwise I'd still be talking to him."

"Are you worried?"

The Music Teacher

"Not very. Carl's mature for his age, and in many ways he's very independent. Only children grow up faster, I think. They spend so much time with adults. I just wish Max wouldn't do those things."

"Like leaving Carl alone? You know, Lydia, this is the first time you mentioned your ex-husband's name. Usually you refer to him as that or as Carl's father."

"Do I? I wasn't aware of it. Perhaps I do think of him in those two capacities rather than as Max the man. Actually his full name is Maximilian, but he was always called Max."

"How did you two meet?"

"At an after-concert party."

"Where?"

"In New York."

"You never told me how you got to New York."

"Now, that's a much pleasanter story." She reached for the brandy bottle. Bernard took it from her hand, which seemed cold, and poured her and himself another glass. She swirled it gently in her glass and inhaled audibly before going on.

"I always loved to play the piano—we do have that in common—and as a child I had some mediocre instruction. Then I went to a girls' college, where I majored in music but didn't learn very much either. As a graduation gift my father gave me money for an extended trip through Europe. Instead, I went to New York to study with that fine Russian pianist whose work I knew from recordings. My father's gift was generous enough that I was able to live modestly in New York for quite a while. And when he found out what I was doing, he was so impressed that he made it possible for me to continue."

"What about Max?"

"What about him?"

"You really don't want to talk about him, do you. You don't have to if you find it painful."

"Not more painful than talking about my sister. If this is to be our evening for getting acquainted, or for exchanging confidences about unpleasant episodes in our lives, or whatever . . . I will tell you about Max. When I met him I went absolutely wild. It was at a ritzy party after a concert by my teacher. He just came over and introduced himself. I had never known anyone like him, certainly not in our little southern backwater. He was suave, elegant, utterly charming. He knew the ways of the world. He spoke languages. He flattered me outrageously. As I think about it now, some instinct in me must have told me at the time not to believe it, but I can't deny that I adored it. He pursued me with the same intensity he had when he went after some business deal. I didn't make it easy for him—my upbringing saw to that—but the more I resisted, the more he had to have me. When he realized that he would have to marry me in order to 'have' me, he did, but he never changed his old ways. I found that out soon enough, just months after Carl was born."

"You said Carl looked like him."

"Yes, but Max is much more . . . dramatically handsome. Perhaps Carl will get that way too when he grows up. I just hope he won't *be* like him. Men don't like the term, but Max is really beautiful. In our first year I often stared at him when he was not aware of it. Everyone was attracted to him; women just flew to him, men loved him. As I once told you, even animals could not resist him. He not only knew it, he expected it. When some minor official or casual acquaintance was cool to him, he had to charm them and win them over, no matter how unimportant they were. He would work at it until he succeeded, as he usually did. It was a real obsession with him."

"How did he make a living?"

"Max considered himself an entrepreneur." She pronounced the word slowly, more like *enterpranyoor*. "He had an office and a secretary, but he kept no regular hours. He invested in this and that; he bought and sold this and that; I never quite knew what. He traveled a great deal, here and abroad, and had endless long-distance telephone conversations, also at home."

"He was a real success, then?"

"He certainly thought so himself. He had no sense of morals or ethics. Any deal that went through was a success, no matter who got cheated. Only people who got caught were failures."

"Did he ever get caught?"

"No, but he came close to it. One time he was being investigated by the district attorney's office. I read about it in the paper and questioned him. He just laughed and told me not to worry. Apparently they couldn't prove anything and dropped the entire matter."

"Tense moments for you, though?"

"Not more than others."

"Did you live in this house with him?"

"Oh, no. We had a large apartment on Fifth Avenue with windows overlooking the park and a summer-and-weekend house in the most fashionable part of Long Island."

"It must have been exciting for you to live in that style."

"It was at first," she conceded, "but to be married to someone you don't really know, you can never know, someone who charms you when he is in the room with you but whom you don't trust for a second when he isn't, someone as slippery as Max—the excitement wears off. I stayed with him because I wanted Carl to have a normal home, whatever that is."

"Why did you finally leave him?"

She hesitated and looked at him through narrowed eyes. "Do you really want to know?"

"Yes, I do."

"I left him when I found him in bed with a man. Please don't ask for any details. I had suspected something like that, but to actually stumble into it was a terrible shock."

Bernard tried to imagine the situation and said nothing. He had read about such things but had never met anyone to whom this had actually happened. She noticed the length of the silence.

"Now that you know all this, do you still like me?"

"Of course, Lydia, and I thank you for being so frank with me."

She put her hands over his across the table. "We did get to know each other a little better this evening, Bernard." She had at last begun to call him that, putting the accent on the second syllable as though it were a French name. "Where do we go from here?"

"Wherever the road takes us, Lydia. We will both know whether or not it is the right one.

He glanced at his watch.

"Do you know how late it is?"

She nodded.

"I'm sorry if I stayed too long."

She shook her head. He got up quickly, kissed her on both cheeks, and left. He could not get to sleep till early morning and wondered whether she was also thus affected.

Chapter 9

FOR THE FOLLOWING SATURDAY, BERNARD HAD MADE A dinner date with Laszlo, the conductor of the local chamber orchestra. They met infrequently but considered themselves friends. Laszlo had come to New York from Hungary and had been quickly absorbed by the musical scene. He was a good violinist and an excellent sight reader, and after several attempts at a solo career or touring with a chamber music group, Laszlo had become what is called a free-lance musician. He played whatever jobs came along, television, commercials, pick-up orchestras for special events; he did not mind, because his dream was to conduct. He did get the position of music director of a community orchestra in Pennsylvania and the local chamber orchestra. Neither position paid much, but they were what Laszlo lived for. If a stranger asked him his profession he always replied, Conductor.

Since the music he had to play on most of his commercial jobs disgusted him, he spent every free evening he had playing chamber music with colleagues in similar situations. He and Bernard had met playing piano quartets at the home of a local doctor. They had liked each other instantly and met again to play or just eat dinner together and talk about music, and they became even closer friends during the rehearsals that led to the concert in which Bernard played the Mozart concerto with Laszlo's chamber orchestra, the concert Lydia had heard.

Bernard wanted to keep his date with Laszlo but did not want to give up his evening with Lydia. He was a little concerned about how the two would get along, since Laszlo sometimes made a negative first impression. As long as Laszlo talked about music he was interesting to listen to and full of insight, but after dinner—Laszlo loved good food and drink—especially if he had had too much to drink, Laszlo would tell jokes, endless, often pointless jokes, many of them vulgar. At the end of each joke, Laszlo laughed loud and hard, as though he had never heard or told that joke before. Bernard treated this as the price to pay for a good evening of music making; he was not so sure Lydia would see it the same way.

He called Lydia first to find out whether she would mind having someone along for their dinner. She was cool to the proposition until she heard who it was. "Oh, I'd love to meet *him*. He looked so colorful on that podium."

Next he called Laszlo to get his reaction.

"So! You got new lady friend. My *dear* Bernard, I am so happy for you. Is she pretty?"

In Laszlo's pronunciation *happy* sounded more like *chuppy* with a hard guttural *ch*, the kind that does not exist in the English language.

"Actually, she's a student," Bernard began to explain, "or on the way to becoming an ex-student—"

Laszlo interrupted him with a guffaw. "You once told me you don't mess with students."

"I don't *mess* with her at all." He tried to keep the irritation out of his voice; Laszlo was sometimes hard to take. "We do duo-piano work on Saturday afternoons."

"Oh, you two play on two pianos." Laszlo made it sound perfectly obscene. Then he became his musician self, thank God, and said, "Any friend of yours is a friend of mine. I will come to your studio at seven, and the three of us will have dinner together. Hey, Bernard! How would it be if I come a little earlier and listen to the two of you awhile? Would you mind?"

"Not at all. Come at six-thirty, please."

He did think it necessary to call Lydia a second time to inform her of this new development. She was thrilled.

"Let's plan to play the Mozart when he gets there," she suggested. "It's our best piece at the moment."

They had worked on the Mozart sonata more than on any other piece and were both fond of it.

"Very good. We'll plan it that way."

Laszlo arrived at six-thirty sharp. He wore a red-and-blue plaid jacket over light tan pants and an elaborate foulard tie. He had always liked colorful clothes, but they were carefully chosen to match and were never gaudy or tasteless. His hair was slicked down with some shiny stuff and his thin mustache must also have been treated with something similar to stay in place the way it did.

"Always prompt," Bernard observed, as he introduced them, and Laszlo raised Lydia's hand to his lips without actually kissing it.

"Musicians must always be," Laszlo expounded to Lydia. "If they are not prompt, they pay heavy penalty. Union sees to that. If rehearsal is called for ten-thirty, this doesn't mean to arrive at ten-thirty; it means you are sitting in your chair, your instrument unpacked, tuned and ready to play. "

"Well, we are ready to play, maestro," Lydia said dutifully. Bernard had told her that Laszlo liked to be called maestro. Only conductors are called that. Without further words, Bernard and Lydia took their seats at the two pianos and played the entire Mozart sonata. Laszlo sat next to Lydia to turn pages for her. He listened to them in silence, occasionally nodding his head as though in approval.

"You play together very well," he said when they finished, "and what a lovely piece! I particularly liked the way you did the ending of the second movement. You know the spot I mean? When you think the piece is over and Mozart suddenly becomes very dramatic, almost like Beethoven. You played that absolutely the way I think it should be done."

Lydia glowed with pleasure.

"You are really a good match, you two," Laszlo went on. "Your ensemble is tops. Perhaps one day you play the Mozart concerto for two pianos with our orchestra."

Lydia could hardly hide her delight. Bernard knew that Laszlo could be facile with words. He would test his veracity later. Lydia had certainly taken to the fellow, or was she just responding to his compliments? She had indeed played well. Bernard thought so too.

They went to a restaurant near Laszlo's house where a big-breasted, broad-hipped woman with an accent even heavier than Laszlo's made the best schnitzel, strudel, and goulash outside Hungary, as he assured them. They drank Pilsner Urquell and talked about pianists, conductors, and music.

Laszlo, whose cheeks had become quite red, almost the color of his jacket, asked Lydia, "Do you know about the cellist who always played the same note?"

Bernard was afraid of what was to come, but there was nothing he could do about it. He sat back in his chair and watched Lydia.

"No, I don't," she said.

"Well, this cellist always played the same note, one note, always the same. When they ask him, 'Why you always play the same note?' do you know what he answer? He says, 'All other cellists are looking for the right note; I'—pronounced more like *oi*—'*I* have found it.' Ha-ha-ha-ha."

Lydia smiled. "Musicians tell such funny stories."

Laszlo went right on. "Do you know the one about Beecham?" He did not wait for a reply. "Beecham was rehearsing Handel's *Messiah* and they come to the passage 'for unto us a child is born'; he thinks the women in the chorus don't show enough enthusiasm. So he turns to the soprano and alto sections and says, 'You must think of the pleasures of conception, ladies, not of the pains of birth,' ha-ha-ha-ha." This last was said with a Hungarian imitation of a British accent.

Lydia looked a little strained, but she continued to produce a smile.

"Now I tell you shortest joke I know," he went on, "not a musical one, and then I must go. I have an early rehearsal tomorrow. A man came into a restaurant and asked the waiter, 'Do you have frog's legs?' 'No,' said the waiter, 'I'm just very tired.'" Another bellyful of laughter.

Laszlo looked around to get the waiter's attention and Bernard gently tapped him on the arm. "Do you really mean it, Laszlo, about our doing the Mozart two-piano thing with the orchestra?"

"Of course I do. Would I have brought it up otherwise?"

As though the effect of all the beer had suddenly disappeared, Laszlo turned to Lydia. "I have admired Bernard's playing for years," he said. "I think he should have had a much bigger career than he did. And I think you two make a very good musical team together. You complement each other."

The moment Laszlo spoke seriously about music, he became a different person. His accent diminished and his grammar became more correct.

"I have another piece of advice for you two," he went on. "If you should decide to play in public together—and I think you should—look into the one-piano four-hands repertoire. Much wonderful music has been written, music that has been neglected for too long. As our professor here, I mean Bernard, will tell you, rising bourgeoisie of the early nine-teenth century liked to make music at home, especially to play four hands on a newly acquired piano. All publishers of that time had music for them. Mozart wrote many sonatas, not just one, for this combination and if you, dear Lydia, don't know the Schubert Fantasy in F minor, you're in for a great treat. It is one of his best works. If you and Bernard bring all this music back to audiences, you'll do yourself, them, and music in general a great favor."

"That was quite a speech," Bernard said, "and you are absolutely right. There is lots of wonderful music in that cat-egory—I have much of it on my shelves—and we will indeed take it up, even if we have no plans to go public with it."

The waiter had brought the check, and as Laszlo was about to rise, Lydia said, "May I ask you a personal question before you go, Laszlo?"

"Not too personal, I hope. What is the question?"

"Do you consider yourself a success?"

"Do I consider myself a success?" he repeated. "I've never thought about it in just that simple way, dear lady. But as I think about it now, I would say yes. Look, Lydia, I got out of Hungary with my fiddle. I make a good living in New York. I have to play a lot of trash, but they pay me well for it. I have two orchestras I conduct—neither of them is the New York Philharmonic—but yes. I think of myself as a success."

"If you think so, then you are," Bernard said.

"Is that really so?" Lydia wondered.

"Whatever it is," Laszlo concluded, "I have to go home now. I have a long day ahead and I need my beauty sleep. Ha-ha."

As soon as Laszlo had left the restaurant, Lydia leaned over to Bernard and kissed him straight on the mouth.

"Oh, Bernard," she said, "I'm so happy! We, you and I, are going to, play solo with his orchestra!"

Bernard, surprised by her sudden kiss, nodded.

"What a strange combination of good sense and vulgarity that Laszlo is," Lydia continued. "When he speaks about music he is so well informed, almost erudite. But then come these ghastly jokes! He's not bad looking either, if he would only stop greasing his hair and maybe shave off that silly mustache."

"I just ignore those things," Bernard came back. "Underneath and behind them Laszlo is a solid fellow and a superb musician. His suggestion of our looking into the four-hand repertoire is excellent. I don't know why I hadn't thought of it myself."

"Next Saturday we were going to have dinner at my house anyway, Bernard. Since we only need one piano for this music, why don't you just come to my place in the afternoon?"

"Fine."

"Will you bring the music?"

"Of course."

"Do bring the pieces Laszlo suggested. Especially that Schubert Fantasy. I'd love to try it."

When Bernard got to Lydia's house on Saturday, several volumes of four-hand music under his arm, she offered him a glass of sherry.

"Even before we play?" he asked.

"Why not? Let's drink to a new episode in our lives: moving from two pianos to one."

When they sat down next to each other on Lydia's piano bench, they became instantly aware of the difference. The proximity of their bodies, occasionally touching when the positioning of the hands required it, the warmth their bodies exuded, even hearing the other breathe—it all made for an intimacy playing on two pianos did not have. There is an element of competition between the players when they are at two pianos, Bernard thought, but when both play on the same piano, they become musically one.

He had put the Schubert Fantasy on the piano rack and sat to Lydia's left in order to take the lower part, a traditional gesture of courtesy which she appreciated and accepted. He had played the piece, though not for many years—he could not remember whether he and his childhood friend Peter had known it—but Lydia was playing it for the first time. Only in the fast middle section did they have to stop once or twice for her to get a difficult passage right.

"You are a remarkably good sight reader," he told her when they came to the last chord.

"Thank you, Bernard, I've always enjoyed reading music as much as studying it. And it's really a gorgeous piece! Laszlo didn't exaggerate when he told me I was in for a treat."

"It's one of the great pieces of all time," said Bernard,

looking for suitable superlatives. "Are you tired, or shall we play some more?"

"I'm not at all tired! Let's do one of the Mozart sonatas."

"Fine."

He opened the music to the first sonata in the volume, a relatively short piece.

"Shouldn't we switch?" Lydia asked. "I mean, shouldn't I take the lower part this time?"

"If you like."

They stopped for an early dinner, a pleasing mixture of cold salmon with a piquant salad of mangos, endives, and tomatoes accompanied by hot rolls.

"Take two of them and butter them hot, as my grandmother would have said." It brought a warm smile to Lydia's face. They drank a light white wine.

When Lydia went to the kitchen to put things away, Bernard took a leisurely look around her living room. It seemed to contain a strange mixture of diverse elements. There was a photograph of her family—he recognized her features easily in the younger girl—in an inexpensive frame next to an odd selection of knickknacks, the kind a young girl might have accumulated over many years. Some of the furniture was elegant, a very comfortable leather settee next to a low marble coffee table with gilded legs. That must have come from her married period, he thought. Other pieces seemed more utilitarian.

What he found puzzling was the array of paintings hung on all the windowless walls; they ranged from sentimental, amateurishly painted flowers to pointillistic visions and totally abstract designs, one of them in a hexagonal frame. Bernard tried to define the personality of the collector who had assembled them. Perhaps there is a story behind every one of them. Someday I will know.

"Shall we play some more music?" Lydia asked when she returned.

"Yes, let us."

He put Debussy's *Petite suite* on the rack and sat down next to her. As they got ready to play, Bernard put his hand around her shoulder, drew her to him, and kissed her fully on the mouth.

"You mustn't do that, Bernard."

"And why not, you southern lady?"

They rose from the piano and he kissed her again, more forcefully this time, while holding her tightly to him. She responded. He turned her around and marched her slowly toward the bedroom, walking closely behind her with his hands on her breasts. He felt her nipples through the dress. When he put her gently down on the bed, she said "Wait a moment. Let me take off my dress so I won't crumple it."

As he took off his own clothes and put them on a chair, he observed how exquisitely shaped she was. She had the same long white thighs his mother had. Was it because of her that he had never liked heavily tanned women?

When he entered her, a slight shudder went through her body.

"Are you all right?"

"Yes, Bernard, it's just that it has been a long time."

She warmed to his caresses, and when it was over she whispered, "I had not planned this for tonight."

"I certainly did not plan it either, Lydia, but it was bound to happen sooner or later. You knew that, didn't you?"

"Yes, I can't deny I had thought about it."

They lay quietly next to each other, thinking about what crossing this threshold would mean to their future together. But neither was ready to discuss it yet.

She rested her head against his shoulder and pulled at a clump of hair on his chest.

"I didn't expect you to have so much hair."

"And I didn't expect you to have such a beautiful body. My God, that sounds wrong; it sounds as though I had expected you to be ugly. What I mean to say is that I was so busy dealing with your mind, your thoughts, and your musicianship, I never even tried to imagine what you would look like naked. It seems like an additional bonus to have you be so lovely. Now that sounds wrong too."

She laughed. "No. I know what you mean to tell me in your sweet, awkward way, and I like it."

A little while later she asked, "If you didn't plan for this tonight, when did you decide to even try it?"

"When you kissed me after our dinner with Laszlo."

"But I just kissed you out of exuberance and joy."

"Perhaps you didn't know it, but it revealed more than that. I do believe there is a moment when a woman decides whether she will have a man or not. I knew at that moment you wouldn't reject me."

"Well, you knew more than I did."

"You mean you just let it happen?"

"You are asking too many questions, Bernard."

She got out of bed and put on a light dressing gown.

"Are you trying to put distance between us?"

"No, I was just a little chilly."

"If you're chilly, come back under the blanket with me."

Chapter **10**

BERNARD AND LYDIA BEGAN TO SEE EACH OTHER MUCH more frequently after that night. He went to her house late at night, when Carl was asleep, and she came to his apartment in the early afternoon, when he was still at school. They dropped all pretense of formal lessons and played together, on two pianos or four hands on one, whenever they felt like it. Carl was often present during their musical sessions. He sat absolutely still and listened when they played. This puzzled Bernard, who had had almost no experience with young children and thought of them as fidgety bundles of energy one had to keep occupied, diverted, squashed, or otherwise forced into silence. Not Carl. He sat quietly in a big armchair, his feet tucked under him or sticking out straight ahead. He just sat and listened. Yet in restaurants or other public places he was as restless as other children.

Bernard and Lydia had grown very fond of the Schubert Fantasy in F minor; it had become a sort of symbol of their new love and they played it often, exchanging upper and lower parts. Then, one day, having just finished the Fantasy, they both went into Lydia's kitchen to prepare a light snack when they heard the opening melody of the Fantasy played in a hesitant but entirely correct way. They both turned around and went to the door: There was Carl, standing in front of the piano—he fitted in easily between the bench and the keyboard—playing Schubert's lovely melody. They froze in their pose at the door and watched Carl come to his first problem. The melody begins on the white keys, but before too long it uses a D flat and a B flat, both black keys. Carl played the D natural, stopped, tried surrounding notes like C and E, and finally hit the D flat and laughed.

"Who taught you that?" Lydia asked her son.

"Nobody taught me. Isn't that what you just played?"

"It certainly is," Bernard affirmed. He went over to the piano, lifted Carl and put him on the bench, and sat next to him.

"Let's play it together," he said. "You play the tune as you just did, and I'll play the accompaniment."

Carl laughed again. "This is fun."

When Bernard played the lower part with him, Carl had to play in time. He hesitated a few times, especially when he needed to find the D flat again.

"Let's do it again," he pleaded.

"Okay."

The second time Bernard did not have to slow down for him at all. He stopped to show Carl how to hold his hand on the keys and how to use the thumb as well as all the other fingers.

"More," the boy kept saying. "Let's do more."

"Not today, Carl. Your mother and I have to go out in a little while. But if you want to, I'll play with you again tomorrow."

"Oh, yes. Please."

Lydia had remained in the doorway and observed the whole scene from afar. When she and Bernard were alone she asked him, "What do you make of all this?"

"I think it is quite extraordinary. I've never seen anything like it. First of all he obviously has a good ear, the way he picked out the notes. He also has a logical mind. Did you notice how he corrected his errors? His sense of rhythm is also sound. As soon as he knew the right notes, he played perfectly in time. I think it all adds up to what we call talent. For some time I've been impressed by the way he listens to us when we play. It is surely an indication of his love for music."

"Yes, he behaves much better than is usual for him when we play."

"I think he should be encouraged, and if you don't object, I'll work with him. You could do it yourself, but perhaps it would be easier for him to do it with a stranger. For me it would be a new experience to observe a musical talent blossom from its very beginning, like watching a young chick take its first steps after it leaves the shell."

"You're not doing this just because he is my son?"

"You saw and heard what he did. Weren't you impressed?"

"I was certainly surprised, I didn't expect it of Carl. Do you mean to say you will give him lessons?"

"We won't call it that, either to him or between us. I am curious. I would like to see how far he will go before some bitter old teacher, or some incompetent young one, ruins music for him."

He remembered the day when Lydia and Carl first came to his studio, how he had been afraid she would ask him to teach the boy and how he had prepared his rejection. Now he was offering to do just that. But then, he thought, I also did not expect us to be lovers when I first saw her.

They went out a great deal together, he and Lydia, mostly to concerts, but also to museums and occasionally to the theater. She scanned the newspapers for events that might interest them and arranged to have tickets. One day she saw an announcement that Grete Winter was singing one of the leading roles at the opera.

"Would that be your Mitzi?" she asked.

"Grete Winter?" He looked at the ad in the paper Lydia had been reading. "So she's gone from Gretel to Grete. I guess the *l* had to be dropped. Too Viennese for a star of international stature."

"You're still bitter when you speak about her. Bitter or sarcastic."

"She's not on my mind much these days, especially since you have come into my life. But my memories of her are not exactly sweet."

"You know what, Bernard? I want to go to the opera to see and hear her. Will you come with me?"

"What a strange notion. I have no desire to see her, but I can understand your curiosity. All right, I'll go with you."

There were no tickets to be had for the first seasonal presentation of the opera Mitzi sang in, but Lydia secured tickets for one of the later ones.

"Shockingly expensive, these tickets," she said.

"Let's go to a movie instead," he quipped. "They're cheaper."

It was not an easy evening for Bernard, sitting in the next-to-last row of the orchestra section, and he tried to make jokes during all the intermissions. Mitzi had indeed grown a little stout, but in spite of what that critic had said her voice sounded as beautiful as ever, he thought, and she still looked damned good.

Lydia wanted to go backstage, and Bernard tried to discourage her. "There'll be a huge waiting line outside her dressing room. She doesn't receive, as she calls it, until her stage makeup is removed, and that takes quite a while."

"Let's just look at her from afar. I've never been backstage at the opera."

They walked through endless corridors past many excited people rushing here and there until they stopped outside the baritone's dressing room. He was bare from the belt up, proudly exposing his manly chest and passing out signed photographs of himself in various costumes to a group of high school girls who giggled in rapid unison.

Farther down the hall an usher opened another door and through it they could see Grete Winter, wearing an elaborate brocade dressing gown, with her hair—still the same color, as that nasty critic had pointed out—hanging freely over her shoulders. With a queenly gesture she accepted the handshake of her first admiring visitor. Bernard did not think she could possibly have seen him, the line was too long and the light in the hall not bright enough. He took Lydia's hand and pulled her away.

"You're pale," she said.

"It's just these ghastly lights." He tried to make another joke. "Next week we'll go to the commodities exchange or the cotton futures markets to watch your Max operate."

Lydia gave him an uncomprehending look and they went home quietly.

Bernard worked with Carl once or twice a week. At his request Lydia was not present at these sessions.

"The boy is making progress," he told her. "He grasps everything so quickly, he knows how to overcome problems, altogether an astonishing talent. On top of it he seems to have inherited your memory."

"All I know is that he enjoys being with you," she said, "and that it's doing him good. He is much more manageable at home lately and his schoolwork has improved."

Roger, Bernard's best former student, was in town for a few days between his Australian tour and some twenty concerts on the West Coast. He called and asked to see Bernard, who gladly made an appointment with him.

"Is he the one whose photo hangs in your studio?" Lydia asked, when he told her about this forthcoming visit and asked her to be present. "Wouldn't you rather be alone with him?"

"No, I want him to know about you. Roger is like an old friend now. I'm sure you'll like him; he's such a delightful, witty fellow. Every time he comes through town between his eternal tours, his wife gets pregnant. They already have four children, and he tells me there is a fifth one on the way."

"Success on all fronts."

"You might put it that way."

Roger breezed in the next afternoon. He was a big-boned young man who seemed to fill the entire room with his presence the moment he entered it, not just physically but with his exuberant spirit. Bernard asked him whether he wanted a drink or coffee.

"Coffee, this time of day," he said and began to tell stories about his Australian tour, describing places, people, and incidents, both amusing and frightening. In between he asked Lydia a few questions, as if to assess her role in his former teacher's life. Soon the talk turned to music.

"On my next tour," Roger said, "I want to play Schumann's *Kreisleriana*. There's a certain passage I have ambivalent feelings about; I can't decide how to do it. May I play it for you?"

"Of course."

Roger went to the piano Bernard reserved for himself—did he remember it from his student days?—and played a musical passage three times, each time in a different way.

"Which of these do you like best?" he asked Bernard.

"I prefer your second version." Bernard went to the student piano and played it, also from memory. "I think it brings out that counter-melody in the middle voice."

"I agree. Thank you, Bernard. I'll do it that way."

Bernard was gratified that Roger still sought his advice: Roger, whose last name was known to music lovers all over the world.

Lydia had kept in the background so far except to answer the questions Roger had directed at her. Now she asked him whether he would be willing to play the entire *Kreisleriana* for them.

"With pleasure," he said, and made the piano sound as she had never heard it before.

"My God, you're good!" she said when he finished. "You deserve every ounce of your success."

"Thanks. Bernard told me you two are playing on two pianos together. You should form a team and give concerts. Call yourselves the Winter-Harding Piano Duo. Or the Harding-Winter Duet Team. Better still: Take the first letters of his name and the last letters of yours, Lydia, and put them together. You'll get the Bernydia Ensemble. Or if you like it shorter: the Bernia Ensemble."

Bernard laughed. "Still up to your old tricks, Roger.

Bernydia sounds like a town in ancient Greece, and Bernia sounds too much like hernia. Both come out better, though, than Lydnard, which is what you get if you take her name first. In any event, we don't have to worry about this until we are ready for our first concert."

Roger had to rush off to some other engagement and left, wishing them success in their future as a team.

"Oh, I'm so depressed," Lydia said, the moment he had closed the door behind him.

"Why depressed?"

"I'll never be able to play like that, no matter how much I practice."

"Hearing someone play who is better than you"—Bernard held forth—"should inspire you, not depress you. Even if you know you can't attain that level of perfection, it should move you to strive for it."

"I don't know," she said. "I tend to react the opposite way. It makes me want to give up; it makes all my efforts seem hopeless."

Bernard put his arm around her and whispered in her ear, "You poor, weak creature." Then, in his full voice, louder than necessary, "As your former teacher let me tell you that this is quite the wrong attitude to take."

She pulled away from him. "Anyway, I do like your Roger. He's such a happy man, and he just exudes energy and warmth. And his hands! Did you notice them?"

"I have known his hands since they were small and weak. Roger deserves his success, as you told him. He worked hard enough for it."

"It must have been a joy to watch his hands grow. It gives me some idea of the pleasures and satisfactions of teaching. You're right, I should be glad to have heard him here this afternoon. And I loved it when he said you and I should do more with our ensemble playing."

"I'm beginning to think so too, Lydia. We must talk about it some more."

Lydia did more than talk about it. A few days after Roger's visit she announced that she had contacted a concert manager, a man who recognized Bernard's name, and had invited him to have drinks with them one afternoon the following week.

"You don't wait for the grass to grow, or whatever the cliché is for such occasions."

"Please be serious, Bernard. I think we *have* a potential, and Jack Bronston, the manager I spoke to, believes there could be renewed interest in two people performing on pianos together. All I've done is take the necessary steps instead of talking about them."

"I've known your name for many years, Mr. Winter," Jack Bronston said, when they met him in the lobby of a hotel on Central Park South where drinks are served, "and I'm delighted that you want to re-enter the concert arena. There is, as I always say, no time like the present."

"The 'concert arena'! What an odd way of putting it.'

"Well, isn't it in some ways like a battlefield? You have to be a little meshugge to enter it." He turned to Lydia. "Crazy. You know, cuckoo."

"I'm not sure I want to enter any arena at this time in my life," Bernard said, a little solemnly.

"Perhaps I'm expressing myself clumsily, but that was the distinct impression I had from the young lady's phone call. Please tell me in your own words what you had in mind."

Lydia answered. "We've been playing on two pianos for

some time, Mr. Bronston, and four hands on one piano as well. We do get along well together"—with a sideways glance at Bernard—"and we wanted to discuss with you the possibility of getting concert engagements as a team."

"Are you two married?"

"No," said Bernard. "At least not yet."

"Does it make a difference?" Lydia asked.

"No, I just wanted to know. Are you planning to do a New York recital?"

"We haven't formulated our plans precisely yet," Lydia explained. "Frankly, we wanted to sound you out on various possibilities."

"Sound me out to your heart's delight, young lady, but remember you will *have* to give a New York recital sooner or later."

"I was afraid you'd say that," Bernard said. "I have been through all this once before."

"I know you have, Mr. Winter. I was a piano student myself when you had your Carnegie Hall debut. I never understood why you didn't give a second concert. Very few people establish a career with just one appearance. I know much more about all this now that I work for management. Talent alone is not enough. As I always say, it takes patience and persistence to build a reputation."

"I'll try to supply those elements," Lydia offered.

"If you do, young lady, you'll be well ahead on the road to being a successful team," Jack said affably. "What I can do for you—I *do* believe in your potential, as I told the young lady on the telephone—is the following: The management firm I work for runs several concert series in colleges and small towns. We pretty much control those series in terms of who goes on them. I could book you on a number of those next season. You could try out different programs without any risk and see how far you can go."

"That sounds like an excellent beginning," said Bernard.

"Your fee would be negligible, though."

"I expected that."

"Good. I'll get onto it right away. Nice to meet you, Ms. Harding."

That night, as they were lying next to each other, Lydia's head resting on Bernard's shoulder, she asked, "Those years between your Carnegie concert and our first meeting, what did you do in those years?"

"They just came and went, it seems now. My calendar was always full: a concert here or there, judging some competition, students old and new. One year I taught at a school in Baltimore and went there two days a week. I gave it up; too much time spent on trains."

"I want to pull you out of this. I want your life to have a purpose again."

"Well, you've made a good beginning in that direction," he said, meaning more than she perhaps realized. "In any event, we'll really try to have a career as a duo-piano team."

She kissed him. "I thought I was succeeding with you only in bed."

Chapter 11

AT THE END OF THEIR NEXT PRACTICE SESSION, AFTER much detailed practice of difficult passages in the Schubert Fantasy, Bernard said, "If we are to give concerts, Lydia, we need to widen our repertoire. I'll go to the city tomorrow and rummage through the shelves and bins of the music stores. Let's see what else there is for us to choose from."

He felt happy in an invigorated, hopeful way he hadn't felt in years, and Lydia must have seen it on his face when he returned from town with a large envelope full of music.

"It looks as though your foraging expedition has been a success," she said.

"Very much so." He pulled the uppermost piece of sheet music from the envelope. It was Robert Schumann's Six Studies in Canon Form, transcribed for two pianos by Debussy.

"Well, well," Lydia said, looking at the title page. "That's a curious find. I wonder whether this was a so-called labor of love for Debussy or whether he got paid by some publisher for doing it. what do you think, Bernard?"

"We could look it up in one of the books. But right now, let's sit down and play it."

Lydia was an excellent sight reader, as he knew, and they played through the six pieces without much difficulty.

"What lovely music!" Lydia said.

"It's Schumann at his very best," Bernard elaborated. "It has the same delicate quality his finest songs have. And that epilogue! Isn't it wonderful for a set of pieces to end in a philosophical, almost elegiac mood? It appeals to me much more than those endlessly repeated chords some composers deem necessary to tell the audience that their music is over."

"But these quiet endings never get the kind of applause the bravura ones do."

"No, they don't, my dear ever-practical Lydia, but I adore the way this last piece ends. What also amazes me about this set is that Schumann never loses his identity while writing canons—after all, counterpoint was not his daily language—and the pieces are all in strict canon. That is something we would expect from Bach, not from Schumann."

"I don't think I'm being overly practical. I was just thinking of audience reaction. And I'm with you as far as early Romanticism is concerned. I can't stand the self-loving everlasting gushings of Wagner or the excessive sweet-sour sentimentality of Mahler."

"Strong words, Lydia. Luckily neither of them has written for the piano, so we don't have to worry about including them in our repertoire. But we'll surely consider this Schumann. By the way, did you notice how we made all the little ritards and accelerandi together, even at first sight? It shows how much of a team we have become."

"I'm glad you think so. What else is in that bag of yours?"

The next piece on the pile was a sonata for one piano, four hands, by Poulenc.

"Do you think I'll be able to read that?" Lydia asked.

"It looks manageable," Bernard replied, while thumbing through the pages.

The piece opened in the most unusual physical position they had ever encountered: the treble player's right hand had to be below the bass player's left. They both laughed when they saw what Poulenc wanted them to do.

"Shall I put my hand behind your back or under your arms?"

"Under, I think."

She had to come very close to him to do it, and he kissed her on the cheek.

"I love this," she said. "We're playing music neither of us knows: our new equality!"

He kissed her once more.

When they finished playing the sonata they agreed that it had wit and charm. They were a little puzzled by its strange alternation of tart, dissonant chords with sweet melodies.

"I wonder when this was written?"

Bernard looked at the last page, which gave the date as 1918. "Good Lord, he must have been very young when he wrote this. I don't remember when he was born; let me look it up . . . 1899; that means he was all of nineteen years old when he wrote this. Amazing, though, it has all the qualities of his later music. I guess personal traits show early in life and don't change all that much later."

"It certainly makes a striking impression on first impact," Lydia said, "but I like it a shade less than you do. I don't think it'll wear well; we'll be tired of it long before our first concert."

"You may be right. Let's put it aside for the time being."

Next he put Pierre Boulez's "Structures" on the piano. "This, I believe, was the last piece he wrote in strict serialism.

After that, even he gave up. I have heard it talked about but have never attempted to play it. Shall we give it a try?"

Lydia bravely read the fearfully difficult first piano part in which single notes were spaced all over the keyboard, their sequence, location, and rhythmic arrangement determined by mathematically derived formulas. After a few pages she stopped and closed the book angrily.

"Please, let's not go on. I hate this stuff. I don't think it's worth the trouble."

To smooth her ruffled temper he put a book of Bach Chorale Preludes before her. They played one of them, "Jesus, Joy of Men's Desiring," which brought tranquillity back to Lydia's mien.

"These are lovely," he said, "but I think we should steer clear of transcriptions of famous pieces in our program, although audiences would probably adore them."

"Aren't we going to play for audiences?" Lydia wanted to know. "Or are we going to play only for critics?

"Being practical again? I hope they'll all be there, and we must find music that will interest and satisfy both."

"Is there much more music in that envelope? I'm getting a little tired. All this sight reading is a bit of a strain, you know."

"I do, Lydia, and you do it so well. Yes, sight reading demands a lot of concentration. How about just one more piece?"

"All right."

He put a new sonata by a young Scandinavian composer on the music rack.

"Not one more of those, please!" Lydia begged.

"This one looks quite different. Come on, let's try it."

It turned out to be a fine piece, both as music and in

its expert writing for the medium of two pianos. Its style was personal without following any of the well-known schools of composing.

"Hey, that's really nice," Lydia said. "How come I've never heard of this guy?"

"You've never heard of this guy because . . . look! I could either give you a lecture on who runs the music business and how corrupt it is, or we could have a cup of coffee to conclude a well-spent afternoon."

"Let's have coffee."

"Let's, but before we do, I think we should seriously consider this piece for our program. I'll check with the publishers on Monday to find out if it has ever been played in New York. If it hasn't, we can call it a 'New York premiere.' That'll do us no harm with the critics."

When they sat down for their cup of coffee, Lydia queried Bernard about his own teacher, the grand old Russian lady. "What was she like? Did she play for you? Did she play well herself? What was important to her?"

"What was she like? I'd say she was jovial but unapproachable; friendly as long as you didn't come too close. She always said—I'm beginning to talk like that manager fellow, Bronston, or whatever his name is—but she did *always* say, Play music, not just piano. She was Russian, you know. What else did you ask? Oh, what was important to her? That we form our own opinion about the meaning of a musical composition and how to interpret it. My fellow students, when handed a new piece of music, used to rush to the record library to find out how it was played by Horowitz, Rubinstein, Serkin, or whoever else had recorded it. She strongly disapproved of that. 'Give yourself a chance to find out how *you* perceive a piece of music,' she would say."

"Did she never play during a lesson, just to demonstrate something?"

"Oh, yes. She did play a phrase for you now and then, but never a whole piece to show how she thought it should be played. She really helped her students find their own way to understanding the music. Actually I try to do the same in my own teaching."

"I know you do, but in truth, when we tackle a new piece, aren't we going to play it the way *you* think it should be done?"

"Not necessarily. If you ever feel that I'm imposing my view, please tell me."

"I will. But you *do* know so much more about music than I."

"That's not the point. Let me try to define what good ensemble playing is—you're getting a lecture after all, poor girl, but you asked for it. Well, here goes: When two people play together as a team, their basic approach to the music must be similar, otherwise their playing can never jell; but neither should they lose their individuality. In two-piano music, for instance, when a phrase is played by one pianist and later repeated by the other, the slight difference in inter-pretation is what makes listening to them exciting. If it were identical, it would be totally mechanical. That's incidentally why a man and a woman make such a good team together."

"You do believe that?"

"Yes, absolutely."

"Let me ask you something: If you listened with eyes closed, could you tell whether a man or a woman is playing?"

"In most cases, yes. Of course there are masculine women and effeminate men. It is the quality of playing rather than the gender of the player."

"The whole thing fascinates me."

Bernard, who could get quite formal, even a little

pompous, on occasion, raised his coffee cup to her. "I drink to you, Lydia, even if it is only coffee. I drink to you to thank you for all the new ideas you've brought into my life. Perhaps I was really getting a little stale."

Lydia raised her coffee cup and clicked it against his. "What you said about me makes me very happy. I drink to *us*. And you could never get stale."

Bernard and Lydia were now fully accepted as a couple and received invitations as such. Lydia attended parents' meetings at Carl's school—she had moved to this suburb after her divorce, she once told him, because the schools were so good—and that led to a number of social engagements. Now that Bernard was deeply involved in Carl's progress himself, he found the discussions of the parents interesting.

Lydia had also stayed in touch with some of her friends from her Fifth Avenue and Long Island days. A few of them had shunned her while she lived alone as a divorcée, but now that she had a man again, invitations began to flow in. Bernard, of course, was a desirable guest on the Upper East Side of Manhattan and was often asked to play. Whether he obliged or not depended upon the manner in which the request was made. One of their hostesses put it this way:

"Aren't you going to entertain us a little before dinner?"

"I'll entertain you even during dinner," he had replied. "I know lots of good jokes."

They were not invited to that house again. Lydia, though she agreed with him that the woman had been foolish and rude, asked him to be less blunt in future. "If we do give a concert," she said, "we'll need an audience—unless you want to play for an empty house—and who is going to come if not our friends?"

"I'll try to be a good boy, but I won't pay just any price to sell a few tickets to our concert."

At a reception on Park Avenue they were greeted by a handsome young woman with the words, "Oh, Mr. Winter! I'm so happy to meet you. I've had your recording of the Schubert B Flat Major Sonata for years and play it often. It would truly be an event for me to hear you play it for us."

There was an ancient-looking Steinway in the corner, and Bernard was afraid it might be a ruin. When he opened the piano, he saw that it had been completely rebuilt, and when he touched it, he found that it had a rich, mellow tone. He smiled at their hostess and played the sonata in an exuberant, joyful way. She thanked him profusely and asked him to sit next to her at dinner. Bernard had read somewhere that in the last century every European brothel had to have, in addition to the small girlish one and the fleshy blond, a Jewish-looking woman. This one would have filled the part to perfection, he thought, with her black hair, her sad, dark eyes, and her skin so white and delicate you could see the veins under it.

The apartment, on the other hand, he found stifling in that heavy middle-European style. There were so many pictures hanging in clusters, so many large art books, so many pieces of sculpture that there was no resting place for the eye. It seemed to him that the apartment, large as it was, could not hold all these accumulated possessions.

Dinner was served on two large tables. Lydia and he were as far apart as possible, and the hostess sat next to him long enough to inform him that she was legally separated, though not divorced, and that her husband and Max had been involved in some business ventures. When she was called away, Bernard sat quietly and listened to conversations around him. The two women at his right were trying to decide which was their favorite floor at Bloomie's, as they called Bloomingdale's; later they compared different brands of sneakers in terms of their quality as jogging shoes. A man and a woman opposite were discussing the price of condominiums in various sections of Manhattan, and at the far end of the table a short dark-skinned man with large protruding teeth was telling in a rasping voice how he had been approached by someone who wanted to clone potatoes and needed capital. "I had the best scientists in the potato world check him out," he told another man, who laughed; they were probably both entrepreneurs, like Max. Bernard never heard the end of that story because the hostess was demanding their attention by clapping her hands.

A large iced cake in shape of a typewriter was being carried in and put in front of a well-known writer whose birthday it apparently was. Everyone sang and applauded as Bernard wondered to what extent Lydia had been part of that world. Did her love of music slumber during the years she pushed a stroller with Carl through Central Park? Did she go to Bloomie's to be rewarded for domestic duties well performed?

In his turn he introduced her to his friend George, the painter, who took an immediate liking to her, and to Nancy, who treated her with some suspicion. George invited them to a party in a loft in SoHo to celebrate the opening of a show of one of his colleagues. They had to take a dirty freight elevator to the floor above the place where the party took place; they had been warned that the elevator did not stop on that floor and that they would have to walk down a flight of stairs, which was better, though, than climbing seven.

When they opened the sliding steel door to the loft, the music that came at them was so loud no further conversation was possible. Jugs of cheap wine stood on tables with paper tablecloths and a variety of junk food in their original plastic wrappers, not even opened at the top. People danced and shouted to each other when they wanted to communicate, but most of them were totally involved in their own physical movement. Bernard remembered a remark by one of the dance teachers at his school. "Dancing," she had said, "began as a group activity; then it was done by couples; now it has become a solitary activity." The dancing here had little to do with the music, he observed, as he watched the crowd shake and contort their bodies. In spite of the barbarically repetitious beat that came out of the aptly named loudspeakers, the dancers created their own rhythms. Perhaps they are all deaf by now, he thought.

Lydia, when he last saw her, had been dancing with a sweating man who had a red kerchief around his head and was holding her loosely by the shoulders. Now she was nowhere to be seen. He discovered a series of small rooms on one side of the loft. The doors were ajar and he looked into them. In one of the rooms marijuana cigarettes were being passed around; in another, stronger stuff was being tried. Sober people sat in the next room, all of them on the floor, and, as is not unusual for painters, they were discussing materials, which ones they liked or didn't and why. In a small room next to the bathroom he found Lydia, a glass of wine in her hand, in an intense discussion with a tall, thin, good-looking young man wearing the official uniform of jeans and a torn shirt. He wore a ring in one of his ears—Bernard could not remember later which it was—and had his long hair tied in a knot, a style Bernard thought had gone out in the sixties.

"So glad to see you, Bernard," she said. "I was looking all over for you. This is Angelo, a young painter and former student of George's."

"Hi," Bernard said, and shook a hand that had not been under a running faucet in weeks.

"You the musician," Angelo said, without any interest.

"I'm the musician," he replied, and went back to the main room, where the music had gotten even noisier. He found a young thing with long unkempt blond hair and danced with her. She snuggled up to him and pressed her well-rounded body against his. Just as he was beginning to enjoy it, a sullen-looking youth in a shirt with many figures painted or printed on it tapped her on the shoulder. "We're going home, baby."

His next dancing partner was a middle-aged woman in an elegant lace dress wearing heavy makeup.

"So glad to find someone my age here," she said and took him by the hand to a relatively quiet corner. "I run the gallery where George exhibits. You're a friend of his. I know you."

Bernard did not know what to talk to this woman about except George's paintings, the only thing they had in common. Lydia and Angelo came upon them in that corner and Lydia, who had come without a purse, asked Bernard to write down Angelo's phone number. "I want to invite him to our concert, if we ever give one."

"Sure," Angelo said. "I love music."

In the privacy of his car, driving through the deserted streets of New York toward their northern suburb, Bernard was reminded of a story his mother had been particularly fond of. It seems that Goethe, when he returned from a party and was asked what he had thought of the people there, had replied, "If they had been books, I would have put them back on the shelves."

He told the story to Lydia.

"You don't talk much about your mother," she said, when he had finished.

"One day I'll tell you more about her. At the moment all I can think of is her fondness for Goethe. She had a volume of his aphorisms, and she loved to quote from it. There was one about the difference between living *with* someone and living *in* someone."

"Oh, that sounds interesting. What did Goethe have to say about it?"

"He says you can live *in* someone without living with that person, and that the opposite is also possible. He says it better, of course."

"Do you remember it? I'd love to hear you say it in German."

"I'll try. Here goes: *Mit jemand leben oder* in *jemand leben ist ein grosser Unterschied.*"

"That must be the opening statement. *Mit* must be 'with' and *in* is obviously the same in both languages. The next sentence is the one that caught my attention. How does it go?"

"Like this: *Es gibt Menschen, in denen man leben Kann, ohne mit ihnen zu leben und umgekehrt. Beides zu verbinden ist nur der reinsten Liebe and Freundschaft moeglich.*"

"And now in English again, please, for me."

"It is not exactly easy to translate Goethe. The gist would be something like: 'There are people in whom one can live without living with them, and vice versa.'"

"Let me think about that for a moment. It's rather deep. Yes, I would agree with it. No wonder Goethe is so admired. Is there more? The quote sounded longer."

"Yes, there is one more sentence. It says roughly: 'To combine the two can only be accomplished by the purest love and friendship.'"

"How beautiful!"

"Isn't it? The last line could also be translated more freely as: 'When the two coincide, purest love and friendship flourish.' Goethe did have wisdom, and no translation does him full justice. Take the word *Wahlverwandtschaften*, for instance, one of my mother's favorite expressions. The official translation is 'selective affinities.' That sounds good but does not come to the core. Actually *Verwandte* are relatives and a simpler translation of *Wahl* would be 'choice.' What Goethe must have had in mind is that people you choose to be with are often better than those to whom you happen to be related by blood."

"Oh, I like that," Lydia said, "and I sure do agree with him, especially when I think of my sister, whom I'm tied to by family forever. Speaking of families, I had a letter from my mother today that really upset me. She writes that my father is infatuated with a young nurse he hired. I've always considered my parents' marriage perfect."

"Are they separating?"

"No, I don't think so. Mother is vague, as usual, but I don't think anything drastic has been decided."

"Marriage was not invented by God, but by lawyers, as a friend of mine says. Think of all the people who swear to stay together till death do them part and a few months later they are in a lawyer's office working out the details of their divorce."

"Marriage is some sort of commitment," Lydia meditated, "like a loyalty oath."

"Look, you and Max swore loyalty to each other. So did Mitzi and I. And here we sit, you and I, crossing the bridge over the Harlem River."

"Bernard." She touched his arm. "These two parties we've been to. Where do you feel more at home, on Park Avenue or in SoHo?"

"Neither. I feel most at home when I'm with you."

"Good."

Chapter *12*

JACK BRONSTON, THE CONCERT MANAGER, CALLED BERNARD to say that he could offer them two engagements, both in the next month. How come so soon and so suddenly? Someone had canceled. No, not a piano duo. A violinist had been taken ill; the office had to fill the dates and it seemed like a God-given opportunity to get them started. Could they have two programs ready on such short notice? Why two? One place was a college in southern New Jersey; there were two concert grands available and the college liked the idea of a two-piano team. The other place was a church in upstate New York which had only one piano and wanted a four-hand concert. Therefore two totally different programs were required. Would that be a problem? Did he need to check with his lady friend and partner or could he assume responsibility? He could? Good. Oh, there was one more thing: Could he, Jack, come and speak to them and perhaps listen to them a little? No, this was not an audition. And, finally, could he bring a friend?

Bernard reported the gist of the conversation to Lydia, who jumped with joy. "That's just what we needed. It's like a shot of adrenalin. Why do you think he did it?"

"Oh, it's surely true about someone canceling. Happens all the time. Many people, some very famous ones, got their first crack at the concert stage because someone couldn't make it for one reason or another. Why did Jack turn to us? With him it's hard to tell. Perhaps to try us out or to give us a chance; perhaps all his other artists were booked on those dates. To us his reasons don't matter."

"True. I do wonder, though, what it might be that he wants to discuss with us. I also wonder what sort of friend he will bring. Probably one of those intense young women with thick glasses and frizzy hair who thrive on the periphery of the arts."

"That didn't sound like you at all. Sounded more like something I might have said. Anyway, I have no idea what our little manager wants to talk to us about, nor whom he will bring."

Jack Bronston's friend was not an intense young woman but a thin young man with red hair who smoked incessantly, lighting a new cigarette from the stump of a burning one before putting it out. Bernard watched him with growing antipathy. Jack wanted to discuss the two programs with them and find out by listening to them what kind of music they played best. He also had to send press material to both places and needed a short biography from them. His office had plenty on Mr. Winter but nothing on the young lady.

Bernard took his upper lip between his thumb and first finger, as he often did when he had to make a quick decision. "We could either lie and invent some history for her," he said, "or simply state where she was born, with whom she studied—her Russian teacher *is* a big name—and that the two of us have just begun to play together."

"I prefer that," said Jack. "Be honest if you can, I always say. The audience will look at the two of you, read the program note, and understand." He smirked. "One more thing: When you two take your bows, don't stand next to each other. The young lady is a little taller, and that doesn't look so good. People have preconceived notions. Some famous movie actors are quite short, you know, but when their leading ladies are taller, they are never seen in a way that reveals that. We can't do that with you two, not on a stage. Just each of you stand on your side of the piano when you get up to diminish the effect."

The thin red-haired young man giggled. Bernard felt anger rise in him and saw on Lydia's face that she also contained herself with difficulty.

"I trust my suggestion doesn't offend you," Jack went on. "It's all in your best interests. I have a lot of experience in such matters, and I know what I'm talking about. I will, incidentally, go with you to these two appearances and see that everything is in order."

"Very kind of you."

As soon as they had left, Bernard opened all the windows to let the smoke out of the room. "Quite a little martinet, this manager of ours. Petulant, too. I bet you this Jack Bronston was born either Jacob Bronstein or Bernstein."

"Don't even *think* that when he's around."

"I'm allowed to make slurs; I *am* Jewish, you know."

"I do, but please remember he's the man who gave us our first engagement."

"That he is."

They made no more music that afternoon. They were

depressed and tense and sought solace in food and drink and in each other's arms. Lydia, who liked to have intimate discussions in the calm that follows lovemaking, asked Bernard to tell her about the women he had known between Philippa and herself.

"All of them?"

"Those that mattered."

"Actually there weren't that many. For several years after my trip to Israel and my Carnegie Hall concert I sought no deep involvements. I had several prolonged periods of depression during which I only wanted to be alone.

"Perhaps I should tell you about my mother. She had similar depressions when she withdrew into herself and did not respond to touch or being spoken to. I watched her often as a boy. In the beginning she came out of these depressions just as quickly and unexpectedly as she went into them; later they became longer and longer. I actually tried to talk her out of her moods. In my childish optimism I thought that if I could only convince her that nothing was as terrible as she seemed to think, she would return to reality. At times she did speak, but then she never knew who I was and occasionally she became violent and destructive. Once in one of her fits she broke a small birthday gift I had laboriously made. My father was very understanding and tolerant. He hired private nurses during her bad periods rather than have her hospitalized."

"What a frightful childhood you must have had, Bernard."

"Some of it was pretty bad. In my early twenties I feared that her illness might be hereditary and consulted several specialists. They told me it was not. I did have my share of depressions, but they always had concrete causes and I eventually pulled out of them. I don't know why I brought all this up just now. I found Jack's visit depressing, but that's no reason to be gloomy. . . . Oh. I brought it up to explain why there were long stretches of time without a woman in my life."

"Your nature is essentially positive, Bernard. At least it seems so to me. You deal with difficulties in a straightforward way, sometimes a little arrogantly, but always effectively."

"My arrogance, as you call it, is really only an absolute intolerance for ineptitude. Coming back to depressions: When you pull out of them, the mood is often one of exuberance. One is full of strength and looking for adventure. In that kind of mood I often began new affairs, but I still avoided real attachment."

"When you say adventure, what do you have in mind?"

"I call it adventure when there is an element of danger present, such as the fear of being found out. I once had an affair with the wife of a minister, and she liked to make love in the basement of his church. That sort of thing."

"Did you really do that?"

"That and worse. What I always found exciting is uncovering a new female body and getting to know the mind that rules it; finding out what the new woman likes and dislikes— you'd be amazed at what some women like. I certainly was."

"Do tell me."

"You might not approve of all the things I've done. Whether a woman is beautiful or not matters much less to me—or to any man, for that matter—than women believe. I've found women attractive whose photo could never have entered a fashion magazine. Those fashion models with their eternal pouting grimaces! Decimated, sexless creatures. I'd never want to take one of them to bed."

"I'm glad you feel that way. I hardly look like one of them."

"Oh, Lydia, you're shaped just right. I love every inch of your body. I sometimes ache just to touch you."

"I hope we'll stay like that forever."

"I do too."

"Didn't you get interested in *anyone*, Bernard, in all those years?"

"It wasn't lack of interest on my part. I wanted to keep people, especially women, at a distance. My favorite line, corny as it is, was 'Don't fall in love with me.'"

"I bet they did, though, especially after hearing that line."

"Some did, I guess, but when I sensed it, I ended the affair. There's no way of doing it without hurting the other person, but when I felt it had to be done, I did it, though not always well."

"You aren't planning to do it with me, are you?"

"Oh, God, no! Don't you know yet that you are totally new in my life, something I had thought would never happen anymore, something I had given up on?"

He had risen to his knees to look at her face, and they were soon engaged in another passionate embrace.

Lydia giggled. "I didn't ask you to make love to me. I asked you to tell me about the women in your life. You still haven't told me anything."

"All right, then, I will. I'll tell you about Ellen. We were together, on and off, for almost three years."

"Does that mean you lived with her?"

"Yes and no. Ellen had an apartment in this very building, two floors above mine. She was a photographer. She had turned one room of her apartment into a darkroom, and there was also a lot of equipment to store. And I, as you know, have my two pianos. For us to move together would have made no practical sense whatever. This way we had a very convenient arrangement. Near enough to get together whenever we wanted to without giving up our privacy."

"Makes sense. What sort of a woman was she?"

"Her looks or her character?"

"Both."

"Ellen had thick black hair and dark eyes; her ancestry was pure Sicilian. She was not exactly heavy, nor would anyone have called her slender. Perhaps 'sturdy' would best describe her, and that includes her character. She had hair on her arms, her legs, and even on her thighs. She was very conscious of that and shaved all the time. Once she even shaved her pubic hair. Am I discussing her looks or her personality by telling you that?"

"Both. Go on."

"Until her hair grew back, life was a little scratchy."

"Oh, Bernard!"

"I thought you wanted to know everything. Ellen thought of herself as being ugly, although in reality she wasn't. But what you believe yourself to be is often stronger than what you really are; it can color your whole life. Ellen had wanted to be a painter, had gotten nowhere, and switched to photography. She made a good living as a photographer—she was a success, as your Max would have put it—but she saw herself only as a failed painter."

"What sort of things did you two do together?"

"You mean in bed?"

"You know that I *don't*, Bernard."

"You probably don't, Lydia, but what kept us together was primarily what we did in bed. Ellen treated sex like a religious ceremony. She lit candles all over the room and even burned incense in one corner. The room was always semi-dark except for the platform bed, for which she had devised some rather fantastic indirect lighting. On those nights she wore a long red gown with many buttons in front that had to be opened one by one. It was like a ceremony. Yes, and . . . and she liked only positions in which her face could not be seen."

"You mean from behind?"

"Yes, even when she climbed on top of me it was always with her back toward me."

"You could never kiss, then?"

"No, but I don't think that is what she wanted to avoid. She did not want her facial expressions to be observed; it was all tied in with her belief in her ugliness. But here I'm making poor Ellen sound like an illustrated page from a porno magazine. She was a kind, warm person and we had some wonderful times together. She still liked to paint, especially landscapes, and during the warm months we often went out on Sunday. She would paint on her small portable easel, and I would lie in the grass and look at flowers and trees."

"You know, Bernard, Max also liked to do it that way. From behind, I mean. Perhaps he also didn't want his face to be seen when he was out of control."

She pulled the blanket up to her chin.

"My God, I never thought I'd ever mention this to anyone."

"Look, Lydia! We've come so close to each other we can talk about *anything*. I know I have not spoken so much and so openly with anyone in years, if ever."

He took her hand and kissed it."

"You've pulled me out of a musical slump and a general slump as well. I think I had unwittingly slipped into a form of 'comfortable obscurity,' as a loathsome professorial colleague of mine once characterized his lifestyle."

"And *you* have been the best thing that ever happened to

me. You know that too. I would probably have turned into a man-hater if I hadn't fallen in love with you. Lord! Now I've uttered it, the sentence that you didn't permit those other women to say."

"Please say it, as often as you wish, and as long as you mean it." He touched her tenderly and stroked her hair.

"Did she work for a newspaper, your Ellen, or did she do portraits?"

"What she did was neither that exciting nor interesting. When I met her she was photographing gargoyles for someone who was doing a book on architecture. She loved gargoyles and would have liked to do her own book on them, but no publisher was interested. Her next assignment was photographing cooked food for color magazines. I never knew how much care is lavished on a photo of some dish of baked spaghetti until I once went with Ellen to a photo session that lasted a whole day and produced just one picture."

"If I were to become a photographer, I think I'd rather work with people, getting their expressions, catching them at an uncontrolled moment, and making them see what they really look like."

"You wouldn't get very far doing that. Portrait photographers, even the ones who don't touch up, have to be flatterers all the time. Very few people want to know what they really look like. Anyway . . . aren't you glad we are in music?"

"I certainly am. And with these two concerts coming up so soon, we'd better get to work in earnest."

"We'll have a double working session tomorrow to make up for today's indulgence."

"Did you say 'double' indulgence?"

"I didn't, but I guess it was."

✿ ✿ ✿

They rehearsed steadily, almost daily, until the day Jack Bronston came in a rather old Cadillac, driven by the red-haired young man with a cigarette in his left hand. They went on the New Jersey Turnpike through an inferno of chemical odors, factory chimneys, and high-tension electric poles, inhaling their driver's smoke until Bernard asked him to open a window.

"You only let in noise and smoke," he said.

"Perhaps some smoke will go out, too."

"Oh, it bothers you." He did not put out his cigarette.

When they got off the turnpike, the landscape became prettier and prettier the farther they went: first suburban, with ever larger plots, and then quite rural.

"I didn't know New Jersey was so lovely," Lydia said. "I thought it was all turnpike."

"I was born and raised not far from here," their driver volunteered. "To me it's heaven."

"Everyone to his own heaven," Bernard muttered.

They were all very irritable when they arrived, but the calm rural mood of the college campus and the elegant modern structure of the concert hall improved their temper. Best of all, the two concert grands were perfectly in tune with each other, as Bernard discovered when he tried them, rushing from one to the other.

"I always see to it that the pianos are tuned just before a concert," Jack said complacently.

Students and older people began to amble into the hall and fill it slowly. Bernard paced back and forth in a backstage room while Lydia sat quietly at a table and did finger exercises on the tabletop.

"What is that supposed to accomplish?"

"Limber up my fingers. My college music teacher taught me that."

"Why not, if you believe in it."

At Jack's suggestion they had prepared a standard program consisting mostly of well-known works. "Give them what they know, what they like, and what they know they like, I always say." These had been Jack's words. "Who was it said, 'No one ever lost money by underestimating the taste of the American public'?" he had added.

Bernard got upset by that quote. "It must have been a journalist who said it." He tried not to show his anger in his voice. "It was certainly not a philosopher or a historian. The percentage of the population interested in real culture has always been small, at all times and in all places. I would say somewhere between three and four percent of the total. Did you know, Jack, that the Vienna in which Beethoven lived and worked had only three hundred pianos?"

Jack admitted his ignorance.

"The majority of the Viennese," Bernard went on, "were not even aware of Beethoven's existence. They never heard his sonatas or string quartets. They listened to their *Schrammelmusik* in their beer gardens."

"Let's not get excited over this, please," said Jack. "I just wanted to make sure your first concert under the auspices of my firm would be a success."

It was. The students liked the Mozart sonata and the Brahms Haydn-Variations, but the greatest applause was earned by Milhaud's *Scaramouche*, a lighthearted, entertaining, slightly jazzy piece written effectively for two pianos.

Even the college music critic, whose review Jack sent them a few days later, thought the Milhaud was the high point of their program. Pity that he misspelled Milhaud as Millaut and that *Scaramouche* became *Scaramunch*. It somehow diminished the value of the entire review for Lydia, though not the pleasure of reading about the "primacy of their pianistic achievement," as the critic had called it. She read and reread a line in the review that singled her out for the "freshness of her approach."

"So he misspelled Milhaud," Jack said. "So what? It's a funny name anyway. No one knows how to spell it. The main thing is he spelled *your* name right, dear Lydia. That's the only thing that matters."

The church concert in a small town in upstate New York was a different kind of experience. Jack begged off going with them at the last minute. Some other event needed his presence more urgently, he hinted, implying its greater importance. Bernard expressed his regrets, perhaps a shade too profusely, and looked forward to a quiet drive with Lydia. It was too long a trip for them to return the same night— maybe Jack didn't want to stay away that long—and he made reservations at a country inn. "Let's turn this into a holiday," he said to Lydia.

The audience was formal, well dressed, and a little stiff. Bernard looked at the back of the printed program and saw that their concert was part of a fortnightly chamber music series that included some well-known string quartets and trios.

"They are letting us know that they are used to the best," he told Lydia, "by being so aloof and cool."

The audience did warm up to the Schubert Fantasy, as any audience would, and a number of people came backstage to tell them they had enjoyed the music and their playing as a team. A few of them added that this was the first four-hand recital they had ever attended. Lydia glowed with joy and engaged many of them in conversation by asking them questions about themselves. It had been a thoroughly pleasant evening, Lydia and Bernard agreed, as they retired to their country inn.

The little town and its surrounding area supported three newspapers. All three of them had sent someone to review the concert and all three reviews were favorable. Under such headlines as POIGNANT CHAMBER CONCERT and DELIGHTFUL EVENING OF RARELY HEARD MUSIC, Lydia and Bernard read that they were a "flawless ensemble" and had given a "hauntingly beautiful interpretation." One critic who ventured into more colorful language and used such terms as "dynamic synchronized propulsion" called them "dramatic sensualists."

Lydia was ecstatic, kissing and hugging Bernard as she kept rereading those reviews.

"Did you hear that, Bernard, we are "dramatic sensual-ists." Oh, I'm so happy! Who knows how far we may go?"

Bernard, more practical this time than Lydia, thought the final line, "We hope they will be back with us soon," more important, as did Jack, who was genuinely impressed.

"This is certainly an auspicious beginning," he said. "But remember what I told you when we first met: Sooner or later you'll *have* to play in New York. You can't build a career on provincial reviews, no matter how good they are."

Well, here I am again, thought Bernard, almost exactly where I was all those years ago. Do I really want to go through this agony a second time? Some things are different, of course, and not just my age. Playing with someone is consid-erably less of a strain on the nerves than being alone out there on that stage. A career in ensemble playing is neither as big nor as demanding as a solo career. But what I have to decide is whether I am willing—no, whether I really *want*—to go into the ups and downs of that life once more. When I did my

Carnegie debut, this town had so many newspapers you could pick a good line from here and there. Now there is only one paper left. It may not even cover the event, and if, God forbid, their review is negative, we might as well quit right then. In a way you put everything on one card even more today than you did when I was young.

All this is somehow tied in with Lydia. I have a feeling, almost a premonition, that if I retreat now, I may lose her. Not that music alone holds us, but it did bring us together and is a vital factor in our lives. Since I met Lydia I have not been in a depression, not a single time. I have come closer to her than to any other human being; I can talk to her about anything; I trust her completely and totally.

And there is Carl. I've grown fond of him since I began working with him. He is progressing at an astonishing pace. He has not only talent and self-confidence; he has that nimbus, that sunny halo the violinist had I went to hear when the violin teacher whose lessons I accompanied came to my shabby room to save me from my worst depression. As a teacher I would like to help Carl grow and be present when he walks out on a stage some years from now. I hope he'll be like that violinist and convince the audience of his being a winner even before he plays.

In different ways, Lydia and Carl have become important to me. Although no priest or rabbi has given us a blessing, we have become a sort of family—perhaps an unusual one, but one to whom Goethe's choice of relatives, his *Wahlverwandtschaften*, certainly applies.

To give that concert or not to give it—don't become too dramatic, please! Go over the consequences of the two alternatives, before you decide. If I do give it, there is no way of predicting what will happen; If I don't—and of that I can be

143

quite sure—if I don't, Lydia's love will diminish and Carl's respect will disappear. Well, that does it!

He called Jack Bronston and made an appointment with him in the same hotel lobby where their first encounter had taken place. Bernard, a little superstitious and sentimental at times, believed that choice of locale was significant when a decision had to be made or announced.

"We've taken your advice," he said to Jack when he arrived, a little late. "We've decided to give a New York recital early next season."

"Good," said Jack. "I thought you would. Congratulations!" They clicked glasses.

"The question now is where and when. Shall we do it in Alice Tully Hall, Merkin, or Little Carnegie?"

"That depends entirely upon how many people you think will come to your concert. There's nothing as depressing as an empty hall. It's always better to fill a smaller house. The other consideration is how much you're willing to spend. This concert will cost you a pretty penny no matter what you do. If you don't advertise properly, don't bother to play, as I tell all my clients. These days it doesn't pay to advertise in the papers. Spot announcements on the classical music stations is what I recommend. That's where your potential audience is. Lovers of classical music are not all readers of newspapers."

"You're probably right. You usually are."

Jack beamed.

"Obviously you, Lydia, and I will have to discuss the details," Bernard went on. "I just wanted to let you know of our decision so we can get things rolling."

"I'll start as soon as you give me the go-ahead. Talk to Lydia by all means, but please make up your minds quickly. These places are booked far in advance. Even now, in late spring, I might not be able to get Tully at a convenient date for you next season."

"I promise we won't waste anybody's time once our mind is made up. Please find out which dates are available at which hall and call me, Jack. That'll help us decide."

"Glad to do that for you, Bernard. Whichever hall it will turn out to be, I think you made the right decision by giving a concert at this point in your Life. Of course you are taking a chance by doing it, but without risk there can be no gain, as I always say."

Chapter 13

BERNARD AND LYDIA DECIDED TO TALK THE WHOLE THING over with Laszlo. He was so much in the midst of musical activity, he would surely be able to advise them. When he returned their phone call he said he was extremely busy with recording sessions but could see them between two of those if they were willing to come to the city. They did and met him at a small Hungarian restaurant on the second floor of a brownstone, where the owner, when he was in the mood and when there was enough of an audience to appreciate it, played Liszt rhapsodies and *Rosenkavalier* waltzes on a small upright piano. The piano was so low he could look over its top to smile at steady customers or welcome newcomers while he played. He even exchanged a few words with guests, as they entered, without stopping to play. That evening the place was nearly empty, which pleased Bernard, who preferred to eat in silence. And they did want to have a serious talk with Laszlo.

They had to wait awhile for any serious talk because

Laszlo, who had already downed a few drinks before meeting them, began the evening with the most outlandish story he had ever told. "There was this group of musicians," he began, "traveling and playing in the East. They come to Baluchistan and play for the king. The king likes very much their playing and says to the majordomo or whatever they call him in those parts, 'Fill up all their instruments with gold coins.' The bass player is very happy, but the poor piccolo player, he cries and weeps. A few days later they play for the Sheik of Arabia"—it would be pointless, Bernard thought, to tell him that there is no such person—"and they play badly. The Sheik don't like it at all and he says to the armed guards, 'Tell them to stick their instruments up their arse'—forgive me, Lydia. The piccolo player says, 'No problem,' but the poor bass player! Ha-ha-ha-ha."

Bernard laughed perfunctorily and said, "It's a good thing they had no piano with them."

To keep Laszlo from going into his next story and to lead the conversation in the right direction, he produced their recent reviews and showed them to Laszlo, who read in silence until he came upon a sentence that puzzled him.

"What does it mean: 'dynamic synchronized propulsion'? Sounds more like engineering words than describing music, ha?"

"We don't know what it means either," said Lydia, "but we think the intent is laudatory."

"Laudatory shmaudatory. I wish they'd say what they mean and say it in a language ordinary humans can understand."

"Please read on," Lydia said. "Later on he calls us 'dramatic sensualists.'"

"Oo-la-la. I bet you like that"—with a broad grin at Lydia.

"I'm a dramatic sensualist too. Don't you think so? We're really of the same ilk. Isn't 'ilk' the right word?"

Not wishing to hear how Laszlo saw himself as a "dramatic sensualist" or where he had acquired the word "ilk," Bernard went straight to the point. "Our manager thinks of these concerts only as a warm-up. He more or less insists we give a New York recital."

"He's absolutely right. This small stuff doesn't lead to anything. So when and where are you going to play?"

"That's what we wanted to discuss with you. We want to do it early next season. Fall is a good time for debuts. Everyone is still fresh, not yet sated by too many concerts. The 'when' is clear to us; it's the 'where' we need to talk about. We can't decide which hall to rent. What is your opinion, Laszlo?"

"To me it's a simple proposition," he said. "If you want to go from small to big, you've got to do it in a big way. Think big, feel big, rent the largest hall you can get. Print big posters, big programs, take big ads in the papers. Make the jump from small to big in one night, no matter what it costs. Who knows when you'll have another chance?"

This sounded to Bernard like a strange reformulation of what he had felt in that inspired, illuminated moment after his concert in the Israeli settlement deep in Arab territory. He recalled the distinct moment which brought him the realization that he needed to channel all his energies into one focal event to propel himself into the active concert life. But he knew that Lydia, by nature and temperament, was more inclined to begin modestly and grow slowly.

He waited for her to speak first. To his surprise she did not comment on Laszlo's remarks but asked him whether he knew any stories about Vladimir de Pachmann. Bernard had observed her reading a number of books about pianists. Whenever she came upon an amusing anecdote, she told him, she made a mental note, planning to surprise Laszlo by playing his own game.

"There are many stories about de Pachmann," Laszlo said. "Which one do you mean?"

"The one I read is where he came onstage and found the piano bench too low. He went backstage, came back with a thick volume of music, sat on it, and found it too high. Do you know what he did then?"

"I think I do," said Laszlo, "but tell it anyway."

"He tore out *one* page of music from that volume, sat on it, smiled, and played his recital."

"It's a famous story." Laszlo went right on. "Do you know the one where he played the Chopin Etude in thirds but left out all the lower notes of the thirds?"

"No."

"They ask him after the concert why he did that. Do you know what he said? He said, 'I saw another pianist sitting in the audience, and I didn't want him to steal my fingerings.' Ha-ha-ha-ha."

Bernard, who had heard both stories before, wondered whether such antics and eccentricities belonged to the last century until he remembered how audiences loved to hear about Glenn Gould soaking his hands in hot water before coming onstage and how they enjoyed hearing him breathe loudly when he played.

Suddenly Laszlo was serious again. "If you're going to give a recital next season," he said, "I'll have you play with my orchestra the following one. This way I'll be able to use your reviews to publicize our concert."

You cautious bastard, thought Bernard, you won't take

any chances on us. No wonder there's a saying, 'If you have a Hungarian for a friend, you don't need any enemies.'

"I'll tell you one more de Pachmann story," said Laszlo. "Then I must go to my next recording session."

Bernard did not hear the final story; he was lost in his own thoughts. He returned to reality when he heard the inevitable ha-ha-ha-ha at the end.

When he and Lydia got back to his apartment, there was a message from Jack saying that Alice Tully Hall was only available on certain afternoons and that he, Jack, did not think an afternoon recital was to their advantage. That left only Merkin Hall and Little Carnegie to choose from.

"Well, Lydia, which one shall it be?"

"Let's do it in Little Carnegie," she said quickly. "I've known that name since childhood, and it would mean much to me to play there."

"Actually it is now called Weill Hall—since its recent renovation—but most people still think of it as Little Carnegie."

The following afternoon Jack came to Bernard's apartment for what he called a strategy session.

"I think you made the right decision," he began, "by choosing Weill Hall. A concert of music for one piano, four hands, is essentially a concert of chamber music and should be given in a hall suitable for such purposes. What we must now decide is *what* you are going to play. Let me elaborate on that for a moment, especially for Lydia's benefit. You have to choose between what is called an 'interesting' program in the profession or a 'standard' one. An interesting program means little-known pieces by fairly obscure composers. The implication is that you do not wish to draw attention to your playing, but rather to the music you are presenting. Many little groups make a decent living by doing just that. The other alternative is that you play major, well-known, standard works. Then you are competing with all the famous artists who play them or may have recorded them—although this doesn't apply so much in your case, since the four-hand piano literature is little known."

"I understand what you're telling us," said Lydia.

"Good. I wanted it to be absolutely clear. My office," he went on, "which is not without influence, will try to plant some articles in the suitable papers about the revival of four-hand piano playing in contemporary New York, and if the sheep read about it in the right papers, they'll come in droves to hear you play.

"In my view the so-called intellectuals of this town are just as much sheep as the lower classes they look down upon, perhaps even more so, because they *read* more. They won't go to a restaurant, buy a book, see a movie, or hear a performer unless their newspaper or magazine has told them to do so. They live fully by what one newspaper and two magazines— all three of them have the words New York in their title—tell them to do and see. I've observed them for years, and I go to enough cocktail parties and after-concert receptions to know. It's really quite funny. On certain days of the week they all talk about the illness of the week, on others they debate the weekly ruminations of the feminist kvetch—a Yiddish term for a complainer, my dear Lydia—they won't take a walk in nature to see the leaves change color in the fall unless they're told precisely where to go. Even the callous hard-boiled moneymen—I meet them too, on occasion—when they read that some dirty Arab has spat into the Persian Gulf, they call their brokers and sell their oil stocks. The next day, when the ocean in Hormuz is smooth again, they buy them back.

"Yet we who love music, we need these intellectuals and

socialites and their pretensions; without them we'd have no concerts, opera, and whatnot. I know that. I also know that if they see themselves as independent thinkers, they're quite wrong. They are just as much sheep, as I said before, as all those others they look down upon: the ones who learn how to live from situation comedies with canned laughter and buy whatever is advertised on television and those teenagers who go mad with adoration over some hideous, half-naked guitar-strumming creature that struts about and yells and screams at them."

Jack's voice had become quite strident. His hands gripped the arms of his chair tightly.

"What is it with you today, Jack?" Bernard asked. "I've never heard you be so eloquent."

"Look, Bernard, as I once told you, I also wanted to be a concert pianist. I didn't make it; I didn't even get near it. Now I'm a manager, a hanger-on, so to speak. I preach to others. I tell them how to succeed at what I didn't achieve."

His voice had gotten quite soft when suddenly the smirk Bernard knew so well by now lit up Jack's face.

"There's one advantage to being a manager, though," he said with emphasis. "If one artist doesn't succeed, we managers just pick up the next one. We never fail for long. Do you see why one becomes a little cynical doing that? Then please allow me my occasional diatribe—I assure you I don't do often what I did here this afternoon—and also allow me my little idiosyncrasies. It's all I have."

He had spoken mostly to Bernard, as though Bernard were better equipped to understand him. Now he turned pleadingly to Lydia. "You didn't mind my lecture, I hope?"

"Not only did I not mind, Jack, I'm truly quite impressed. I'll give you a lecture in return, a more personal one. When I first met you I knew right away that you were smart and that you were good at what you do. You seemed like the born manager. If that's the impression you want to give, you certainly succeed. But now that I know you a little better, I see the man under the guise of the manager. I see him as a deeply disappointed person trying to make sense of what he sees around him."

"Thank you, dear Lydia. I'll always remember what you said. Many people use me. Few know me or want to know me."

His voice had a slight quaver. He cleared his throat.

"Now, back to the question of what you're going to play, the question I asked before my digression. Have you thought about it?"

"I know what I want," said Lydia, "but perhaps we should let Bernard speak first."

"No, dear, we have the same rights here. I have a notion that your ideas aren't all that different from mine. To be absolutely fair, let's do the following: You and I each take a piece of paper and write on it the pieces we would like to see on our program. Let's put them in order of preference. Then we'll hand those pieces of paper to Jack, who'll act as a referee."

Jack liked that tremendously, and when he opened two neatly folded slips of paper a few minutes later, he saw that both of them had put the Schubert Fantasy first and a Mozart sonata second. The only divergence in their proposal was that Bernard had put the Poulenc next and Lydia had written down the Scandinavian composer's name, the unknown one whose music they had read at sight and liked.

"This is an easy afternoon," Jack announced. "You two are so much in agreement, it almost scares me. All right, you want to go for the big standard works. Fine with me as long as you know what the consequences may be. Don't tell me someday I didn't warn you."

"You did, dear Jack, in a memorable speech."

"Let's forget that, please, Lydia. I don't know why I got so carried away. What I need to impress upon you is this: Don't think practicing between now and the concert is all you have to do. You have to mobilize all your friends and acquaintances, so we can fill the hall. I've managed debut recitals for some poor creeps from out of town, and we had about twelve people in the hall. Very depressing, I tell you."

"We do have friends," said Lydia, "and while they come from very different worlds, they're loyal to us and will surely make an effort."

"We'll mix them thoroughly," Bernard added with a smile. "Can you imagine that unwashed painter we met at George's—what was his name, Angelo or something equally unfitting?—can you imagine him sitting next to your lovely friend from Park Avenue?"

"Felicia Weissman? She may like Angelo. He isn't all that offensive, you know."

"As long as he comes to our concert and has taken a shower during the preceding month."

"Okay, okay," said Jack. "I sense an undertone of animosity here. We don't have time for that. You get on with what you have to do. I and my office will do the best we can to make your concert a success."

"Thank you, Jack."

"I've really changed my mind about Jack," said Lydia, after he had left, "and I meant what I said to him. At first I thought he was a dried-up piece of work, unpleasant, cynical, a little obnoxious. Now I feel sorry for him. He's really a deeply disillusioned man who is trying to be *near* music since he can't be *in* it. He's given us good advice; he has strong opinions and a sharp tongue. I wish he'd find a better friend than that cigarette-smoking creature who drove us to New Jersey. That fellow gives me the willies."

When Bernard and Lydia mentioned their proposed concert to friends, all of them expressed delight and offered to help in different ways. George said, "If you give me a hundred announcements of your concert, I'll post them in all the art galleries of this city." Felicia Weissman said she would give them a lavish party after their concert. "All my friends will want to come to the reception. They'll have to go to the concert first."

And Lydia had a letter from her mother:

> Your father has had the sense not to break what we have built over thirty-seven years. That floozy nurse is gone. All's well again and we want to come up and hear you play in Carnegie Hall. We're so proud of you. All our cousins, some of your old classmates, and many of our neighbors have gotten together to charter a bus and come to your concert. As of this moment there are thirty-six of us. We reserved rooms in a motel in New Jersey. It's cheaper this way. Everything has been worked out. Please hold thirty-six seats for us, good ones.

"You thought we'd have a mixed audience," Lydia said to Bernard. "Wait till you see what came in the mail today."

"I think that's beautiful," he said, after scanning the note. "To think there are that many people who love you enough, Lydia, to spend two days on a bus to hear you play."

"It's not just to hear me. They want to be present at an event."

"Don't belittle it. All these people making such an effort. It makes me feel really good."

Lydia had a new dress sewn for the concert. It was made of a light material and fit the contours of her body tightly, revealing her arms, strong and firm, and the faultless skin of her neck. The dress ended where the gentle swell of her breasts began. Bernard kissed that spot and the back of her neck when she tried the dress on for him.

"You look absolutely ravishing," he said. "So beautiful people won't be able to pay attention to your music; they'll just be staring at you."

"Don't be silly. Oh, Bernard, I'm so apprehensive and nervous. Do you think it'll go well?"

"Of course it will."

The last weeks before the concert they practiced daily. It was mostly Lydia, who wanted to go over potential problem spots again and again. Bernard warned against the dangers of overpracticing as he saw them.

"There's no guarantee that we won't fluff that spot," he said, "no matter how often we run through the passage. There's even a psychological possibility of messing it up *because* too much advance attention has been given it. More importantly, Lydia, there's an acute danger in practicing too much: the danger of losing spontaneity. It is better to give an inspired performance with a few wrong notes than a flawless one without spark."

"You're probably right," she said. "I'll just feel more secure if we do it a few more times."

"All right, then, let's do it again."

It was a slight dilemma for him. He often felt they had

done enough work on the program and should leave it alone. On the other hand, he didn't want to prevent Lydia from practicing as the tension mounted in her the closer they came to the date of the concert.

They had decided to spend the night before at a hotel near Carnegie Hall. Thus they would avoid having to travel the day of the concert and would be able to practice at the hall and get better acquainted with the piano they had selected in the Steinway basement a few days earlier. When making the reservations, Bernard had added the night after the concert to their stay at the hotel, so he could enjoy the party Felicia Weissman had planned for them without having to worry about staying sober enough to drive home.

Finally, the evening of the concert came around. Although their hotel was just a short distance from the hall, they took a taxi to protect Lydia's delicate shoes. "You don't ever *walk* to your own concert," Bernard said.

They got to the little backstage room half an hour before the concert was to begin. Jack was already there, wearing a double-breasted suit of some shimmery silvery material.

"You must have lots of friends; we sold almost every seat in the house. If just a few more walk in from the street—did you see the big poster outside?—we'll be sold out. My office has heard through the grapevine that the paper *is* covering the concert, which is a compliment to you two, since there are at least five other musical events in this town tonight. I assume they'll send one of their younger critics. The big guys, as you know, must cover the big events."

You didn't have to say that, thought Bernard; you're back to your old snide ways. Lydia apparently had not heard him. She was sitting quietly on a chair, turning the pages of the music as if to check whether they were all still there. Bernard

was surprised at his own calm. Was it because he was sharing
the perils with another person or was it his age and experience? He looked at his receding hairline in the small mirror
in the bathroom. At least I've kept my teeth, he thought. He
flashed them at himself, white and healthy as they were.
Lydia was still turning the pages when he returned. Her face
was whiter than he had ever seen it. Especially under her eyes
all blood seemed drained. She stared at the music.

"Are you all right?"

"I suppose so. I don't really know." She sent a wan smile
in his direction.

Jack was also back in the room. "Just play as though you
were at home entertaining your friends, young lady." He had
reverted to calling her that. Bernard touched her hands. They
were icy. He rubbed them slowly between his own.

"Oh, Bernard, I love you so." She had never said that to him
when they were dressed or when other people were present.

"Just keep on loving him," Jack injected, "he needs it. But
right now, please put your mind on your piano."

"I will. I will. I will."

At ten minutes after the hour, a sweet young girl in
usher's uniform came in and said, "I've rung the bell and
darkened the house lights. Are you ready?"

She held the door open for them as they stepped out onto
the stage. In the dim light Bernard could see that the hall was
almost full. It was too dark to recognize faces, but he thought
he saw two of his former students in the front row.

Bernard remained calm throughout the Mozart and the
Schubert. He heard himself play and felt totally in control.
Not so Lydia. She was stiff, almost mechanical. Many of the
finer nuances of interpretation fell by the wayside, had been
forgotten, or were simply not realized. There was a rigid

expression on her face. She did not even smile when they stood up to take their bow. Is she going through what I experienced at my debut? he wondered.

Backstage, during intermission, he hugged her. She was still as pale as before and her hands were as icy.

"I don't know what's the matter with me," she said. "I don't seem to be able to concentrate. My fingers are doing what they're supposed to do, but my mind is not there with them."

He took both her hands in his. "I know you're nervous, Lydia, but you've got to turn this anxiety into energy, positive energy. You mustn't let it hamper you. You *can* control it, you have to, and only *you* can."

She let out a deep sigh. "How does one gain control over oneself?"

"By doing it. There's no other way. By willing it."

The young usher returned to tell them that intermission was over.

Lydia's playing got better and better during the second half of the program. It was as though a cloak of ice were being removed from her slowly. In the final piece she was at last free of all inhibiting fears and played with gusto, enjoying the music and the moment in her life.

The applause was warm. They played the two encores they had prepared and could have played one more. Jack, who was the first to come backstage, approved of their not playing a third encore. "Leave them asking for more, I always say." He kissed Lydia on the cheek. "I think it's a smashing success. The audience loved it; I could tell from the way they responded. I just wish the critic had stayed for the whole concert, but one of the ushers saw him leave during intermission. They often do that. It means nothing. Don't worry."

When Bernard and Lydia arrived at Felicia's apartment—
everyone else was already there—one of his students went to
the piano and played the opening melody of the Schubert
Fantasy in the manner of a triumphal march. The guests
laughed and applauded their entrance as though they were a
royal couple.

Felicia's party was indeed lavish. There were tables laden
with exquisite dishes, hot and cold, served by a uniformed
staff who must have been selected for their good looks as well
as for their courtesy. All the things money can buy, thought
Bernard, but he was pleased. Would he have preferred fried
chicken wings, Cheez Doodles, and potato chips?

Everyone there wanted to speak to him. Lydia had gone
to the other end of the room to be with her family and
friends, he assumed. Nancy, George's wife, was first in line.
She gave him a kiss, heavy with dark clinging lipstick, and
said, "This was the most perfect concert I've ever heard. You
two become truly one when music combines you." Two of his
students just shook his hand; they were either too shy or too
dumb to speak. Perhaps they didn't like the concert but had
to show they had been there. Next came Angelo, the painter.
He wore a green shirt with a yellow tie and a coal-black
jacket. "Good music, man," he said.

There were others whom Bernard knew only slightly and
he listened to all of them, vaguely curious whether they would
exaggerate like Nancy, hoping to endear themselves, make
some neutral or feeble comment to hide their true views, or
describe their own reaction to the music at length and
boringly. Only two people were absent: Laszlo, who had an
all-night recording session, and Lydia's older sister, who had
sent a telegram the night before: SORRY. PREVENTED FROM
ATTENDING DUE TO CHILD'S ILLNESS. Lydia was not surprised;

she had never expected her sister to make the trip to New York in a bus just to hear her.

A very good-looking older man approached Bernard with a woman by his side who could only be described as having gone to seed. Before the man even opened his mouth, Bernard knew he was about to meet Lydia's parents. She looks so much like her father, he thought. Good for her.

"I'm Dr. Harding," the man said, "and this is my wife, Ginny. We're Lydia's parents."

"I thought so."

"We came to tell you how happy we are that you took on our daughter as your student and had her join you in this wonderful concert."

Don't they know what Lydia and I are to each other, or is this some variant of southern manners? He chose to give a safe reply. "Your daughter is very talented. You must have discovered that early."

"She did always like to play the piano," Lydia's mother said, "but I never hoped to hear her in Carnegie Hall, not even the little one. I'm ever so glad we came up for this occasion, and we do want to thank you, Mr. Winter, for having brought her out."

A peculiar way of putting it, he thought. There were more people waiting to speak to him, and Lydia's parents had to return to their motel across the river.

Bernard was drinking champagne, which always went to his head quickly, even more so this night, as he was tired and had not eaten anything. The uniformed staff had replenished the champagne glass in his left hand all evening, but he needed his right hand to shake the hands of his well-wishers. Finally there were no more and he rushed to get a plate of food and went to express his thanks to their hostess. Felicia was standing in a corner talking animatedly with Angelo. They were discussing a recent opening.

Felicia had liked it, but Angelo was explaining to her at great length that the man's work was outdated and no longer worthy of her attention. She seemed glad to see Bernard and said in a very soft voice, "You played beautifully, I thought, but Lydia didn't seem to come into her own until the second half of the concert, just before the last piece."

"You are a good observer," he replied, "and I thank you for your honesty. I didn't know it was that apparent."

"I don't know who else noticed it, but I felt it strongly."

Suddenly the room emptied and he could take an utterly exhausted Lydia back to their hotel room. He helped her take the lovely dress off and she fell asleep instantly.

Chapter 14

THERE WAS NOTHING IN THE NEWSPAPER DURING THE NEXT two days. On the third day after the concert, Bernard's phone rang a little after eleven in the evening. It was George. "I hate to be the one who brings you bad news, but perhaps it is better to hear it from a friend than from a stranger."

"What's the bad news?"

"I just bought tomorrow's newspaper and they're discussing your concert. It's not bad for you, but I'm afraid it's terrible for Lydia."

"Oh, my God. What does it say?"

"Want me to read it for you?"

"Yes, please do. I can't get the paper around here until tomorrow morning."

"All of it or just the section that concerns you?"

"All of it."

As he listened tensely to George's voice, Bernard first heard a lengthy discussion of the nature and quality of four-hand music. The young critic dwelt on the fact that it was originally intended for music lovers to play at home and concluded that the level of amateur performance must have been very high at the time, since major composers contributed sizable works of substance and intricacy to the four-hand literature. Only in the last paragraph did the critic mention the performers of the evening. He called them an ill-matched pair, and his final sentence was that Mr. Winter's smooth, sensitive playing was in sharp contrast with Ms. Harding's, who, he stated categorically, was not equipped musically or technically to do justice to the artistic demands of the music.

Bernard was too stunned to say anything to George except to thank him for being a friend. This was the worst it could possibly be. Not only did it devastate Lydia, it also set them against each other by that unfortunate comparison. Bernard walked agitatedly up and down his kitchen, trying to decide what to do about Lydia's reading the review when his phone rang again. It was close to midnight.

He heard a child's voice. "Is that you, Bernard? My mom is very strange. She sits still and doesn't answer when I speak to her. What shall I do?"

"Stay with her, Carl, and don't let her leave. I'm coming right over to your place."

When he got to Lydia's house he found her sitting on a straight chair in a pose similar to his mother's at the onslaught of a bad depression. The technical term was catatonic, he remembered.

"Lydia, it's me, Bernard. Lydia, do you hear me?"

She ignored him as his mother had on many occasions.

"Lydia, don't take this silly review seriously. It's just one man's opinion. Everybody else loved your playing, and they all thought we make a wonderful team."

No response.

"Lydia, we can surmount this thing. It's just a temporary setback. I love you; together we are strong. We can survive it. Please, Lydia, listen to me."

He knelt in front of her and kissed her gently on the forehead. She opened her eyes and looked at him.

"Oh, Bernard, I just want to die. I don't ever want to go out again and see people. I don't ever want to play the piano again."

He knew better than to argue with her. He had often tried unsuccessfully to argue with his mother when she had jumped to unreasonable conclusions or decisions. Carl stood next to him, watching with the instinctive insight children have.

"Lydia," he pleaded, "are you going to let one young man's opinion decide whether your life is a success or a failure? One young man, probably just out of college, trying to show off his recently acquired knowledge; one young man with pimples on his soul, if not on his face? He left during intermission— remember, Jack said one of the ushers saw him leave—he never heard you when you played your best. Lydia, please listen! We *will* play again. There will be other reviews; we've had some good ones, after all, even if they were out of town. Don't you remember Jack telling me that you don't give up after just one concert? You play again."

She remained in her stoic pose. Should he call a doctor? He would only get an answering service at this hour. Should he take her to the emergency room of the local hospital? They would pump some chemicals into her that it might be difficult to wean her from later on. He decided to stay with her and watch her. There seemed to be no immediate medical danger. Carl was watching him rather than his mother, waiting to see what he would do.

"Don't be afraid, Carl," he said to him. "Your mother will

pull out of this, I'm sure. When something bad happens to people, they sometimes react like this. I have seen it before, with my own mother. It won't last long, believe me. In any case, I will stay here with the two of you, no matter how long it lasts. Please go back to bed now, Carl. I will take care of everything."

"I don't want to go to bed, Bernard. Can't I stay up just a little longer?"

"Of course you can. You can stay up as long as you like."

He stroked Lydia's hair gently, but she did not seem to feel his touch. She continued to stare into a distance of which neither he nor Carl were part. He remembered a similar look on his mother's face before she would begin to speak on one of her trips to imagined territory. He remembered waiting as a child to find out where her mind had taken her. He must have looked like Carl, standing there full of fear.

"What happened, Carl? Can you tell me what happened?"

"The phone rang, Bernard. It woke me. When I heard my mom shriek, I came out of my room. She said 'Thank you for calling' to someone named Angelo and hung up. I asked her who was calling so late. She said 'A friend. He gave me bad news.' I asked if Grandma or Grandpa were sick and she said, 'No, nothing like that. Just go back to bed. I'll tell you tomorrow.' Then she sat down on that chair. I've never seen her be so white. I asked her 'What's the matter, Mom?' and she didn't answer. She sat so still, I got scared and called you. I'm glad you're here. Will she be all right again soon?"

"I think so. She's strong and healthy. Sometimes when people get bad news or something shocking and unexpected happens to them, they turn white. Sometimes they even fall over and lie on the ground without moving. That's scary to watch. It's called fainting. Your mother didn't faint, Carl, her eyes were open and she did talk to me once. That's why I think she'll be all right again soon."

Carl nodded but did not look entirely convinced.

"You might as well know what her bad news was," he went on. "The newspaper said nasty things about her piano playing. The newspaper comes out late in the evening in the city—here we don't get it till the following morning—and she must have asked Angelo, who lives in the city, to call her when he saw the review."

"Why did the paper say nasty things about my mom?"

"We don't know why. They sent a young man to write about the concert, and I guess he didn't like her playing. It's true, she didn't play her best that night, but it was certainly not as bad as that critic made it seem. I know she waited with real fear for that review in the paper."

"Did you see it—the review, I mean?"

"No, but someone called me and read it to me, just a little while before you called."

"Was it very bad, the review?"

"Yes, it was. Listen, Carl! Some people react more strongly to disappointment than others. Your mother had hoped to read nice things in the paper, the kind of reviews we have gotten before. I know what she's going through right now. It's sort of the body's defense against mental pain, if you know what I mean. My own mother had similar moments. I remember watching her. It doesn't last long, usually; tomorrow morning she'll be back with us. Now I think she's gone to sleep. There's no reason for you to stay up any longer. Let me tuck you in. I'll stay with your mother all night."

When he returned from Carl's room—he was glad he had calmed the boy a little—a humming sound was coming from

Lydia's lips. You could not call it a snore but rather an inter-mittent hum. Her eyes were closed. He lifted her out of the chair and, although her eyes never opened and she never spoke, her feet collaborated and allowed him to walk her into the bedroom, where he took off some of her clothes, put her down, and covered her. What had begun as a humming sound had turned into a moan, which seemed to emanate from her innermost depths. He stood next to her bed and watched her. She is going through intense pain, he thought, but she is not going the way my mother went. She is too sound for that. Perhaps what I told Carl will come true and she will pull out of it soon.

He sat in a chair from which he could watch her face. She was quiet now; the moan had subsided but there was a deep vertical furrow on her forehead. How frail, how fragile our lives are, he thought, how much at the mercy of others. This terrible sentence, flung down easily by a callous youth, this one sentence in a newspaper which everyone reads, could drastically affect the life of this lovely young woman, lying here in her disturbed sleep. If it has an adverse effect on her—as it is likely to have—it could demolish me as well.

Is there such a thing as getting a second chance in life? Until this evening he had fully believed it. Everything had moved forward and upward from the moment Lydia had entered his studio some months ago: their playing together, their becoming lovers, the beginnings of a career as a team. Only three days ago, at Felicia's party after the concert, Jack had raised his champagne glass to both of them and had said beamingly, "Well, my friends, you can consider yourselves successfully launched."

The possibility of a pianistic career together had been within their grasp, and now—what will happen now? I am a little older and have known disappointment, but poor Lydia, will it destroy something in her? There is no knowing how deeply she is hurt until this depression is over. By taking care of her I seem to have postponed my own depression. I wonder whether I'll get away with it and for how long. Seeing Carl stare at his mother, fascinated, a little horrified, but unable to leave, brings back an image of myself at his age, as though life were repeating itself in some predetermined way. Carl is so talented; we must step aside and hide our grief to let him develop. But we must not give up our own lives and live entirely through him either.

I have reached an age where a sudden heart attack or some horrible disease could come upon me without any warning. I cannot let time run by me as though it were worthless. I have had two chances at a pianistic career and two chances of making a life together with a woman. I lost Mitzi because she was too successful; am I to lose Lydia because she was *not*? Is there some perverse force that runs our lives with irony, or is it all accident and only we perceive the irony of it? Now I am thinking like an adolescent.

Lydia had opened her eyes. "Bernard?"

"Yes, my love. Just go back to sleep. I'm staying here with you."

That was a good sign, quite different from his mother's waking up and thinking she was someone else or not recognizing him. Lydia is not losing her mind. I wonder, though, whether her love of music is strong enough to help her overcome this setback or whether she will turn against music in her rage and pain. There's little one can do for others in such crucial moments. Such decisions are made in their innermost selves, an area no one—parent, lover, or child—can ever get near. Now I'm singing a hymn to solitude! Will you never grow up, Bernard?

It was now four o'clock, the oft-mentioned darkest hour of the night. Lydia was sleeping quietly, and he rested his head against the back of the chair. . . .

The ringing of the telephone woke him. He looked at the clock, which showed a few minutes after nine, and answered. It was Felicia. She had just gotten the paper—it was probably delivered to her door and read during breakfast—and wanted to give Lydia words of consolation and encouragement. When Bernard told her what had happened, she said, "I'm coming over immediately, Bernard. First of all you surely need some rest yourself, and then women are better at this sort of thing."

When he protested she told him there was no stopping her and she was already on her way. She did arrive half an hour later. Carl was pleased to see her. Lydia was still asleep.

"Will you please go home now, Bernard?" she said. "You look exhausted. Just go home and rest. Please! You look so awful, it frightens me."

Bernard expected three students that afternoon. He would either have to call them to cancel their lessons or be there to receive them. He knew Lydia was in good hands. Felicia had proven before that she was a good friend.

"What about Carl?" he asked. "I suppose it's too late for him to go to school."

"Do you know what school he goes to?"

"Yes, I do. I'll call them right away and explain why he won't be there today."

"Good. He and I will keep each other company until Lydia wakes up. Go now, Bernard, for God's sake! I'll call you this evening or if there is any change in her condition."

"Do you think I should call Carl's father?"

"What on earth for?"

Bernard put on his coat, bought the newspaper at a

newsstand, but did not open it until he was in his studio. "An ill-matched pair" . . . What right had he to say that? "Not equipped musically or technically to do justice to the music" . . . How cruel and unjust! This idiotic comparison. We didn't compete with each other, we played together. And this attack on her is a slur on me, her teacher, for having let her play in public. Was she really that bad? She seemed frozen during the first half, but she recovered and played damned well after intermission. By then the bastard had already left. What if there had been no review? Jack would have considered that a failure on his part, but they could have gone on, at least in a modest way. But now?

His students came and went in succession. He tried to concentrate on their playing and made comments now and then so they would not notice that his mind was not with them. Soon after the last one left, Felicia called. "She's up and about. She has taken some food. We are looking through some magazines at the moment. No, she doesn't want to speak with you. Yes, I'll stay the night. No problem."

Bernard was listless. He decided to call Lydia's ex-husband after all. Perhaps Max would want to take Carl for a while. He looked through the phone book, first under Pappasian, then under Papasian. There was indeed a Maximilian Papasian with an Upper Fifth Avenue address. Bernard dialed the number. A deep voice answered immediately. When Bernard tried to explain who he was, the voice interrupted him. "I know who you are, Mr. Winter. I've followed Lydia's life closely since we parted."

"Do you know about the concert we gave?"

""I do, and I saw the review. I can imagine what state Lydia is in. She never took defeat well. All her life revolves around success."

This was a surprising bit of information. Was Max making it up to turn the tables on Lydia?

"I just thought—" Bernard said feebly.

"Look, Mr. Winter." Max had cut him short again. There was anger in his voice. "I don't know why you called. Whatever it is, don't expect too much from me."

"I thought Carl might need you."

"I'm going abroad tomorrow. Lydia has many women friends. They'll help. Good-bye, Mr. Winter."

That was that. Felicia must have known that Max would be brusque and negative. What about his saying that Lydia's life revolved around success? Puzzling, to say the least. This phone call certainly had done nobody any good.

Bernard was exhausted but could not fall asleep. He got up again, poured himself a glass of Scotch, and sipped it slowly. This should do it. He had another and went back to bed. Still no sleep. Thoughts raced each other through his mind, unpleasant thoughts. He got up, fetched the whisky bottle, and put it on the floor next to his bed, not on the night table, so he would not knock it off later. He had a drink straight from the bottle, turned from his right side to the left, then back again, and had another drink, Screwing the cap back on the bottle was beginning to be difficult. As his mind became gradually more and more clouded, he went into a rage. First against Jack, his smugness, his cynicism, his low opinion of mankind, the certainty that Jack would drop them after this review. The next swig from the bottle turned him briefly against Nancy, who never let George or anyone else finish a sentence. He wiped the reminder of her insincere kiss off his cheek and turned more strongly against Laszlo, good musician but terrible person, his eternal anecdotes, his use of the commonest clichés, his cautiousness, and the hideous guffaw after each joke. He dozed a little, but the rage continued and did not let him sleep. He no longer bothered to replace the cap on the bottle, just left it open on the floor. The next swig set his blood to boiling. He was railing against Mitzi, all the years he had spent helping her with her career while neglecting his own. He shouted at her. Had she been in the room he would have struck her. Finally his rage even turned against Lydia, for having propelled him into this turmoil, for having dragged him from his quiet life and then let him down at the moment that counted. But even at the height of his drunken rage there was an element of sanity left that told him not to turn against her and to stop reaching for the bottle. The next sound he heard was the telephone.

It took him a while to get there. His head had a ring of iron around it, his walk was uncertain, and the taste in his mouth could only be duplicated in a cesspool.

It was Laszlo, apologizing for calling so early, but he had to rush off. He was telling him not to be upset over that review, life was tough, only the strong survive, they should ignore it and go right ahead with another concert, and he would always be his friend. Thank you, Laszlo.

Perhaps a cup of coffee would help, or a grapefruit with its tartness. They didn't. I'm getting too old for such drunken bouts. They kill brain cells; that's about all they accomplish. He knew of only one medicine that would remove the cesspool taste from his mouth: it was named Bach. He went to the piano, took out a volume of the Suites and Partitas, and began to play some of his favorite movements, a prelude here, an allemande there, a few sarabandes, and not so many gigues. Suddenly he came upon the prelude Lydia had played for him that first afternoon. He closed the book and took out Schubert sonatas. They had a similarly purifying effect on his soul. He played the one in B flat major that Felicia had told him she liked. As he continued to play, the effects of the alcohol began to wear off and his inner life returned slowly to a state of normalcy. Music will always mean more to me than anything else, he concluded.

Two days later Lydia was in his apartment. She had not announced herself, but she was familiar enough with his schedule to know when to find him alone. She wore a simple skirt and a sweater, and while still pale she looked her usual self.

Without any small talk she went to the bedroom and, while standing in the doorway, she turned to him and said, "I'll be in there waiting for you. I want you to make love to me." He took his clothes off and followed her. She was lying naked on her back.

Bernard went to lie beside her and began to stroke her gently. Her eyes were closed. He touched all the parts of her body that had been dearest to him, the soft skin on the insides of her thighs, that little roll of fat on the upper curve of her hip, the skin around her nipples . . . she remained quite still. As he proceeded further—an erect penis has no conscience, as the saying goes—she moaned a little as though he had hurt her. There was no stopping now. Except for raising her knees slightly, she remained as still as ever. He was reminded of the story of a group of musicians who went on tour with an inflatable doll looking like Marilyn Monroe. They all masturbated with that doll and, as the story had it, one of the musicians had syphilis and all the others caught it this way.

Here I am, he thought, doing what she and I have done so often together, and doing it all alone. When he was finished, she patted the back of his neck. "My poor Bernard. I do love you, though. You know that?"

He was lying quietly-beside her. This had always been her favorite time for intimate or serious discussion.

"Lydia, dear, dear Lydia," he began. "I can't tell you how glad I am that you came. But what you did just now was an act of will, not an act of love. If we are to overcome what that newspaperman has done to us—I still maintain we gave a damned good concert—if we are to go on together, this is not the way to do it. We need to be gentle with each other, talk, make music, and let this wound heal."

She listened to him in silence.

"Come again tomorrow, Lydia. Come in the early afternoon. First we'll play together on two pianos, perhaps something new, something we've never played before. Later we'll have a bite to eat and then—"

"No, Bernard." She interrupted him. "We'll never make music together again. I've made up my mind. I will *never* touch a piano again."

"I know how upset you are, but isn't that rather extreme?"

"Don't you understand what this has done to me? I've always doubted the extent of my musical talent. You did encourage me and I loved you for that. But that fellow on the newspaper told me the truth. I now believe him, not you anymore."

She got up, turned on the light fully, which made her eyes seem more metallic than usual, and put on her clothes. Her face was sharp and determined, strangely old and childish at the same time.

Should he try one more time? He loved her enough to do it. "What about the pleasure of making music, Lydia? Just making music for the joy of it, without plans, without any thought of success or failure? Making music the way we did a few months ago?"

"You can't go back in time like that. What happened *has* happened. I'll gladly continue to see you, Bernard, but I'll *never* make music with you again."

Fully dressed now, she came over to the bed where he was still lying naked, kissed him on the forehead, and went out.

He stayed in the same pose, naked on his bed, and tried to assess what had gone wrong. Should he have stopped the lovemaking when he realized it was not an attempt to resume their life together but rather some demonstrative, symbolic gesture on her part? Probably. Was her self-esteem more important to her than music? Apparently. Perhaps her eroticism was somehow tied to power and success, and now that these were gone, at least in connection with him, her body had rejected him? Pursuing that theory, he remembered the first time she had ever kissed him had been after Laszlo had told them they'd play with his orchestra—that would surely not happen now. The second time she had hugged him on her own initiative had been when Jack announced that he could offer them two concerts. Was he being too harsh on her in his own anger and disappointment? He was only trying to be honest with himself.

Had she come to his apartment to make love or to tell him she would never play with him again? Perhaps she had made that decision during the act? He would never know unless they had another intimate discussion, and the likelihood of that was remote. Would he ever hear from her again?

He did. She called the following day and said, "Carl has some sort of vacation at his school, and I'm taking him with me for a visit with my parents. Carl absolutely insists on having a lesson with you before we go. He says he won't go with me unless he sees you first. Can you fit him in?"

"Of course I can, Lydia. Let me look at my little book. If you can come tomorrow at six, you'll be my last appointment for the day. I'll have unlimited time for both of you."

"Thank you. Carl will be very happy."

She brought him, but did not stay to listen. "I have some shopping to do before my trip. When shall I come to pick him up? An hour from now?"

"Fine."

Carl was already playing little pieces from Bach's Anna Magdalena's *Notebook*, "The Happy Farmer" and others by Schumann, and some music by Kabalevsky that he liked particularly well. Bernard was fascinated in seeing the young mind grow faster than the young fingers. Never having taught a child before, he now realized that he had deprived himself of a deeply satisfying experience. Carl, unencumbered by false beliefs and imposed habits, went to the essence of the music he learned with a purity, agility, and directness that astounded Bernard. When something was unclear to him, he asked astute questions, and he was always willing to accept guidance.

That afternoon Carl looked as though he had cried earlier in the day. "I don't want to go to South Carolina with my mom," he said. "I want to stay here with you and play the piano."

"Is there a piano at your grandparents' house?"

"Yes, they have one, a dinky one."

"Dinky or not, you can practice on it. I tell you what: I'll give you a list of pieces you can work on while you're there. I'll number them so you know in which order to take them, and I'll write on this piece of paper what I think you should pay special attention to in each of them."

"If I have a question, can I call you?"

"Any time. Now listen carefully, Carl. There are several things I want to talk to you about today. First of all, your mother: She's had a very hard shock, as you know, and she needs time to recover and come back to herself. Going away for a while will do her good. So will staying with your grandparents. You must be especially good to her during these coming days. I know you are young and you think older people are there to protect you. But sometimes a child has to protect a grown-up. As I told you when we watched your mother the night she wouldn't speak, I went through something very similar with my mother when I was about your age. I was sometimes angry with her for being as she was, but most of the time I tried to help her. You have to do the same for your mother now."

Carl nodded. "I will, I promise."

"Good. The other thing I want to talk to you about is your music. Don't let it swell your head, please, when I tell you that you have a wonderful talent for music. Anybody can learn to move his fingers correctly; anybody can learn to read music, to use proper fingerings, to pedal without blurring, and other things, but talent—you either have it or you don't. Nobody can give it to you. And you, Carl, you have it. Always keep that in mind, especially when you're sad."

He waited a moment to let it sink in.

"The last thing I meant to tell you is that, if your mother doesn't object, I will be your teacher until you're grown up. That's an absolute promise. Unless, of course, you would want to leave me."

"Never, Bernard."

There was so much conviction in Carl's voice, only Bernard's ingrained reticence and his acquired professional demeanor kept him from embracing the boy.

"We still have a few minutes before your mother comes back. Have you heard from your father lately?"

"He's in a place called Brazil. Mom says he's in some kind of trouble and won't be back for a long time."

"I see. Play the Kabalevsky once more. There's a spot you can do better. I'll stop you when you get there."

As he listened to Carl's playing, it occurred to him that if he and Lydia were to separate completely, he might never see Carl again. I must not let this happen, not only because of Carl's talent—others could teach him just as well—but because he is the closest thing to a son I have ever had and probably ever will have. My brief conversation with Max convinced me that Carl cannot "expect too much" from his father either. In a way he needs me as much as I need him. Yet I have no means of holding him or keeping him.

Lydia was remote and polite when she came to collect Carl. Bernard went out for a lonely dinner with a whole bottle of wine.

The next morning's mail brought a letter from Jack Bronston's firm of concert management. It included a detailed list of expenditures and a total of income from the sale of tickets. To his surprise Bernard learned that they had ended up in the black; they had actually made a little money on the concert. How absurd! How totally absurd, this drop of success in that ocean of failure. Yet he couldn't stop giggling over it. He went to the phone to chat with Jack and thank him for everything, but when he identified himself to Jack's secretary, she said, "Mr. Bronston is on the other line. He'll call you back, Mr. Winter, as soon as he gets off."

He never did.

Chapter *15*

BERNARD'S LIFE RETURNED SLOWLY TO ITS NORMAL PACE. He devoted much of his time and thoughts to his students. Harrison, the intense boy who always wore a white shirt and a tie to his lesson, was struggling with a modern piece of enormous difficulty. Music to him was a series of challenges. As soon as one was surmounted, the next one loomed. Bernard often wondered what pleasure Harrison got out of music itself, or whether his main satisfaction came from conquering difficulties. In his way he will go far, though, Bernard thought. He will probably write a book someday that very few people will understand, some analytical treatise a few devotees will revere and the rest of mankind will happily ignore. Bernard did not expect Harrison to make his mark on the concert stage, but he enjoyed working with him, even if it meant having to argue every small point of analysis and interpretation.

The full-breasted girl without hips was not making any progress at all. She was doodling around with the same few dreamy pieces. What she needs, thought Bernard, is a shot of something or other, or else she will doodle away her entire life. I ought to have a so-called serious talk with her, the kind that will make her cry a little, to pull her out of this lethargy, but I am too tired for that today. I have had two such talks with her in the past, and the effect lasted only for a few lessons. She is an essentially placid creature. Before too long she will get married and play for her children on rainy Saturday afternoons. Still, there will always be music in her life.

Bernard had set aside an afternoon to audition new students. Some wanted to work with him; others came to play for him and sought his advice. He was often asked to reach conclusions quickly or make decisions for them, decisions that might vitally affect their lives. There was a call from an older man who had said on the telephone when asking for an appointment, "I've worked for an insurance company all my life and played the piano every free evening. Now I'm about to retire and will at last have the time to devote myself fully to music." When he listened to him play, Bernard knew almost immediately that the man was extremely limited—how quickly one recognizes talent or the lack of it—and had severe rhythmic problems. Bernard recommended books to him that might be helpful and sent him to a former student of his, a woman who had a special knack for helping people with precisely circumscribed problems.

Next came a young woman who at first sight looked a little like Lydia. Only her colors were similar—she was in fact quite different. "I want to play for you, Mr. Winter," she said, "to get your advice. My friends tell me I'm equally talented for music and for painting. I can't make up my mind which to pursue."

Even before he listened to her, Bernard told her, "That is a decision only *you* can make. I certainly can't make it for you; I don't know your paintings and I am no expert in that field anyway. The only advice I can give you is that you should be guided by what you *enjoy* more, music or painting, rather than by what some people think you are talented in. Allow me to lecture for a moment: Your choice of profession is one of the most important decisions you will have to make. You will spend more time with your profession than with anything else, or anyone else, for that matter, including your future husband. Therefore you must choose the activity, the field of the arts in your case, that gives you the most satisfaction to spend your time with. That was not a good sentence, but I hope you understand what I mean."

"You've already helped me, Mr. Winter. The way you put it has clarified my mind. I don't even need to play for you anymore. If it's a question of what I prefer, I know I'd rather spend my time painting. I love to sit and look at things, to mix colors and try to get it down right. I have more patience for that than for practicing the piano, repeating some difficult passage over and over again. Thank you, Mr. Winter."

How different from Lydia she was. As she walked into his studio he had observed that she had fat legs, quite unexpected under that slim face. He refused her offer to pay for his time, saying with a laugh that they had spent little time together and that his advice was worth either a million or nothing.

Next came an ebullient young man. "Thank you so much for seeing me, Mr. Winter. I do hope you'll have time for me. May I tell you why I'm here?"

"I think I know, but tell me anyway."

"Well, it happened like this. I went to a concert of a young pianist. He came through my hometown and gave a big concert. I had never, but never, heard anyone play so well. Then I read the program notes. It said that he had studied with you." Must have been Roger. "I knew then and there that I *had* to study with you. I sure hope you have time for me."

"Do play something for me. What did you bring?"

"I've been working on the 'Goldberg Variations.'"

Bernard liked young people who tackled objects larger than their ability allowed them rather than those who smugly repeated what they knew well.

"Well, well," he said. "We may not have time for all of them. May I pick the ones I'd like to hear?"

"Certainly, Mr. Winter."

"Begin with the theme, please."

Even the technically rather simple theme of the "Goldberg Variations" revealed a singing tone in the right hand, an elegance of mind in the execution of the ornaments, and a distinct feeling for the long line. (How quickly one recognizes talent or the lack of it.) Bernard picked some of the more difficult variations, and the young man handled all of them with aplomb.

"What else do you have in your fingers?"

He played some Liszt, revealing a fiery temperament and considerable technical brilliance.

"You're quite similar to my former student Roger, when he was your age," Bernard told him.

"That's the nicest thing you could have said to me, Mr. Winter. Will you have me as a student?"

"I will indeed. I look forward to working with you. Tell me a little about yourself. Shall I call you James or Jim?"

"Please call me Jim, Mr. Winter. Everybody does. Well, I was born and raised in Michigan, in a small town near Muskegon. My mother is a piano teacher, my father sells farm equipment. My mother went to the famous Music School in New York. Now that I think of it, you and she might have been classmates there, Mr. Winter."

"What was her name?"

"Wrigglefield. Mildred Wrigglefield. That was before she married my father."

"I may have known her, although I don't remember at the moment." Would I have forgotten such a name?

"Anyway, she taught me ever since I could walk. I learned to read music before I learned the alphabet. I never had another teacher. But when I heard your former student play, Mr. Winter, I went to my dad and told him I had to come to New York and study with you in order to play like him one day."

"There's no guarantee of that."

"I don't want any guarantees, Mr. Winter. I just want to play the piano and play it well."

Listening to Jim and talking to him improved Bernard's mood considerably. So did a letter he found in his mailbox that day, a letter from Italy inviting him to be a judge at the same competition he had won in his youth. The other judges were well-known pianists and eminent teachers. To be listed among them flattered him immensely.

In the evening Bernard went to a concert at one of the smaller music schools in the city. A former student of his, a girl named Eisenberg, had formed a trio with two other young women, one a Wasp with long blond hair, the other a slender Japanese girl. They had invited him and would surely ask for his comments after the concert. The blond girl held her violin rather coolly but produced enchantingly mellow sounds; the Japanese handled her cello as though she were making love to it, and little Tara Eisenberg, his former student, dramatized each musical phrase with her entire body. He had tried to cure her of that, thinking it was an affectation, but had left her alone when he realized how much a part of her character it was.

As he listened to them, he mused how these three temperamentally different young women could make such excellent chamber music together. He also observed how little racial origin seemed to matter these days, and he was glad of it. When he was a student, there would have been either a Japanese trio or one of three little Eisenbergs. He also remembered, without any obvious reason, how, during his stay with Mitzi in Vienna, they had gone to a concert together and the man behind them—it helps to know the local language if you enjoy eavesdropping—had carried on about how Marian Anderson, an American Negro, could never understand the music of "our" Schubert. Thank God, nobody thinks that kind of nonsense anymore.

Bernard received an invitation to an opening from a gallery in SoHo. The work of Angelo Buonagusto, it said. So his last name is Buonagusto, a nice last name to have, especially if you are an artist. The show embraced a period of three years and was called a "mini-retrospective." They used to have retrospectives after something like thirty years of painting; now it takes just three years to entitle you to one. He has probably been painting for only four years. That was nasty, Bernard. What do you have against the young man? He looked at the date on the invitation. It was three weeks hence. He jotted it down in his appointment book.

On the Sunday before the opening of the exhibition, the newspaper had a long article about the show. It carried a photo of Angelo—he looked extraordinarily handsome—and next to it one of his pictures, which consisted entirely of circles, repeated endlessly.

Bernard began to read. The article opened with a discussion of postmodernism, which was described as "yet another way to define the world without God." (Aren't we done with that yet? Oh, well, a word is a word is a word.) His eye began to skip and fell next on a sentence that said, "Painting is a polyvocal art." Laszlo would love that! It stopped again on the "demystification of the concept of universality." (I wonder whether Angelo even knows any of those words.) Then the article quoted a painter whose name Bernard did not recognize as saying, "Great art does not dwarf all other art . . . it throws the admirer into a state of crisis." (Would I want my listeners to be thrown into a state of crisis?)

Finally, the article got around to Angelo. He was only twenty-eight years old. He had been born in the South Bronx, had been through a drug rehabilitation center at age sixteen, and had begun to paint only recently. (I suspected that.) When Angelo was interviewed, he had said, "Nature does not interest me. People don't interest me. The beautiful as such is not what I strive for." (I hope you'll find happiness with your circles. You certainly seem to have found success with them.) When asked whether he considered his art "geometric," he had answered with a disarming no, which enchanted the writer of the article to no end. To the question what he would do with his money, if he were suddenly rich, Angelo had replied, "I would arrange to have talented kids from underprivileged neighborhoods get free painting lessons." (The first thing that has a ring of truth to it.)

The article continued by praising Angelo for his modesty and self-restraint by using only black and white. It ended by comparing the "visual rapture" of repeated circles to the "aural ecstasy" of repeated musical phrases, through which some of our composers of recent prominence had succeeded in combining the avant-garde with the popular.

Bernard called his friend George to find out how such an article comes about. "Oh," said George, "I saw the piece too. You're naive, Bernard. Do you really think the art world is any less corrupt than the business world? It needs new products constantly, and if there's nothing extraordinary around, they elevate something quite common to that status."

"That doesn't explain the whole thing."

"You haven't let me finish. The crux of the matter is this: People who buy a painting by an unknown *before* he gets big are likely to make a lot of money. You can compare them to manipulators with insider information on Wall Street. A painting, after all, has no absolute value. Its price is simply what the market will bear, and that is often determined and controlled by gallery owners in collusion with the press. I've put it rather bluntly, but that is approximately what's going on. Today's new product will, of course, be discarded with equanimity tomorrow."

"Aren't you annoyed or repelled by all this?" he asked George, whose speech reminded him of a similar one by Jack Bronston, his former manager. "You talk about it in such calm tones."

"I've seen it too often to be excited anymore," George continued. "I accept it as a fact of life. Aside from all this stuff, I like Angelo. He's a nice kid and he had a terrible childhood and adolescence. I'm really glad they picked him as their next object of adoration. As long as *he* doesn't believe all this crap himself, he'll be all right."

"Sure," said Bernard, who was not so convinced that Angelo was a nice kid. "Will you be at the opening?" he asked George.

"You bet I will. Angelo worked with me for a while, as you know. Even if I didn't want to go, Nancy would drag me there. She thinks Angelo is cute."

"I'll go too, George. I'll see you there, and thanks for your explanation."

When Bernard arrived at the gallery, it was so crowded he had difficulty getting in. As he pushed his way gently through the throngs, he realized it would be impossible to get near the pictures. The people there simply blocked them. They didn't seem to mind, either; even the ones closest to the pictures often had their backs to them. They all talked animatedly with one another. Bernard understood that after the article in the Sunday paper one just *had* to be at that opening and one had to be seen being there. Sprinkled among the elegant connoisseurs were a few youngsters in jeans. They must have been Angelo's friends from earlier years. They formed little groups here and there and were totally ignored by the art lovers.

Bernard had always enjoyed eavesdropping. As he moved slowly around between clumps of people, he heard snatches of conversations. "Isn't it marvelous how he evolved from squares to circles in less than three years? . . . I admire artists who reach maturity early."

There was a thin young woman with a large black felt hat pulled right down to her eyebrows. "To me circles are mandalas," she said. "How wise of him to see that. And repeating the circles is a true hint at eternity."

The effete young man with her, in a leather coat with golden buttons, offered his comments in a pinched, nasal voice. "Circles are eternally feminine. Yet Buonagusto is so profoundly masculine."

Only one old curmudgeon whispered something under his beard about the "emperor's new clothes." Being pushed as well as working his way forward, Bernard found himself near a table with good French wines, served out of bottles, not jugs. There was not much left, though, and all the food had been eaten, which was surprising since the people present did not look as though they couldn't afford a piece of cheese on a cracker.

He decided that he had had enough and was about to leave when he suddenly came upon Lydia. She stood, a few feet away, right next to Angelo under one of the larger pictures. It gave him quite a pang. He stopped where he stood to gather himself. Lydia was looking up to Angelo. She had to, since he was almost a head taller than she. She was speaking into his ear while he gave her his attention only occasionally, being engaged in shaking hands with well-wishers and accepting their flatteries.

As soon as he had recovered from his initial shock, Bernard went straight to Lydia to confront her. "I didn't know you were back in town."

She looked at him as though he were just another visitor at an art show. "I've been back a couple of days. I was going to call you. Carl wants to continue his piano lessons with you."

"Is there some place around here where we can talk for a moment? In private, I mean."

"Yes, there is."

She led him to a small room in the back. There were metal desks in it, file folders, and an addressograph. It must have been the gallery owner's office. Lydia sat down in a swivel chair, turned it around, and faced him. She wore a light blue dress that underscored the color of her eyes. They were hard and impregnable. Bernard remained standing in front of her, like an applicant for a job. "You've been back in town for two days and haven't called me?"

"Three days, to be precise."

She crossed her legs as if to tempt him with a glimpse of her thighs.

"And why not?"

"Because I have nothing to say to you."

She had not tried to tempt him at all; she had just wanted to sit more comfortably.

"Lydia, what has happened to you?"

"Nothing has happened to me. I've had a little time by myself and have thought things over."

There was a small painting on the wall, just above Lydia's head, a realistic painting of a young girl. It must have been left over from some other show. He stared at it numbly as he listened to her.

"Look, Bernard, while I was down there at my parents', I decided that I would have nothing more to do with you, musically or otherwise."

"But why, Lydia? Because of that silly review? Or because of that strange night?"

"That strange night, as you call it, didn't help, but it goes deeper."

The girl in the painting on the wall had the beginnings of a grin on her face, a malicious grin. Is this what it feels like to be in a doctor's office and be told that you have some fatal illness?

"You have hurt me very deeply," she went on. "I don't think you even know *how* deeply."

"I didn't mean to hurt you, Lydia. I thought we went into this together. We could have won together, but we lost together. Why can't we go on together?"

The girl in the painting was grinning openly.

"Let me tell you what you did to me, Bernard. First you

built up my confidence; then you destroyed it. You raised my hopes—I trusted your judgment of my abilities and potential—then you led me to disaster. Was it just because you liked to go to bed with me?"

"No, Lydia. I did not raise your hopes because I enjoyed making love to you. I truly believed in your talent. I still do."

The girl in the picture was now laughing out loud; he could almost hear her. Lydia got up from her chair. Her face was very close to his.

"Don't you understand at all, Bernard? You took me up a tower. When we got to the top you told me I could fly. I believed you. I jumped off the tower and fell. I fell flat on my face in front of hundreds of people. I will never forgive you for this, never. I hate you! I truly do!"

Her voice had risen to a pitch. A little saliva had escaped her mouth and landed on his forehead. He wiped it off with the back of his hand. *At least Mitzi never shrieked at me. She never told me she hated me, either. She just went where the grass was greener.*

"I still don't know why you have turned against me, Lydia, but I suppose I have to accept your decision."

"Yes, you do."

"Then there's nothing more between us?"

She shook her head, sat down again, and turned the swivel chair so her back was toward him. The gesture could not be misunderstood. He had turned to leave when she called him back, her voice quite low and artificially calm.

"There *is* one more thing between us, Bernard."

"What?"

"There's Carl. He wants to continue studying with you, he absolutely insists on it. You know how strong-willed a child he is."

"I also know how talented a child he is."

"Just don't lead him up any towers! Don't do to him what you did to me."

"That was unnecessary, Lydia . . . quite uncalled for."

"Well, will you continue to see him?"

"If that is what he wants, yes."

The girl in the painting had returned to her serious mien. Lydia seemed to be staring at some papers on the desk. Bernard left the little office, hoping to get out into the street quickly, but he was cornered by Nancy. George stood next to her, talking to some people.

"Don't you think the boy has a terrific future?" Nancy asked.

"What boy?"

"Angelo, of course, you dumbbell."

George took him by the elbow and introduced him to his friends. Bernard made no attempt to know their names.

"Are you a painter also, Mr. Winter?" one of them asked.

"Yes," he answered, without having heard the question.

"Are you drunk or something?" Nancy asked.

At this moment one of Angelo's pictures must have been sold. The gallery owner was sticking a little red star on the frame of it. Lydia went up to Angelo, raised herself on her toes, and kissed him when the sale was announced. Some people applauded.

I'm sure she won't lie there like a piece of wood when *Angelo* climbs on top of her. He now hated her too. He had not done anything deliberately to hurt her. He had not taken a single step without consulting her. Why had she turned against him so totally? He hoped she wouldn't turn Carl against him also. The way she had phrased that question about his leading him up a tower and having him fall to his death. Was he really a murderer in her eyes?

The Music Teacher

George, Nancy, and their friends were engaged in a serious debate, so serious that Bernard managed to get away from them without being noticed. If he had bid them good night, they would surely have asked him to have dinner with them. He needed desperately to get out.

As he went down the hall he ran into Felicia, who was also leaving.

"I don't know what all the fuss is about," she said.

"What do you mean?"

"Oh, Angelo and his circles and squares. They bore me to tears."

"Me too."

They walked a block or two without speaking.

"Lydia is acting very strangely since she's come back from her parents," Felicia said.

"I don't think I want to talk about Lydia."

"What do you want to talk about?"

"You, Felicia."

"What is there to talk about?"

It came out like an old recording. "I liked you the moment we met. I'd like to know you better."

"That can be arranged."

There I go again, thought Bernard. Soon I'll be telling her, "Don't fall in love with me." She'll answer, "Your warning is coming too late. I already have." And the game will begin all over, the old game I know so well. Is that what's in store for me now? A new student, a new woman, some new music?

"Will you have a drink with me, Felicia?"

"With pleasure."

It would be better, much better, than that open whisky bottle on the floor next to his bed.

Chapter *16*

A FEW WEEKS AFTER ANGELO'S OPENING AND THE DISASTROUS encounter with Lydia, Bernard had a phone call from Laszlo.

"I have something I want to discuss, something important."

Bernard could not imagine what that might be, but he saw no reason to refuse Laszlo. He had not heard from him in a while and was pleased that Laszlo's silence—reasons for which could easily be found—was not permanent.

"Glad to. When and where?"

Laszlo mentioned a Czech restaurant on the Upper East Side of Manhattan. Bernard had heard of it. Czech food meant duck and dumplings to him and he was not fond of either. There would be other items on the menu, though, and if it was a restaurant Laszlo frequented you could be sure it would be good.

Laszlo took food seriously. Not that he was a glutton; he was much too vain to overeat. But he did like to eat well; he considered it a mark of civilization. Once Bernard had said to him, "I'll take you to a good Mexican restaurant," and Laszlo had given him a lengthy lecture. "That, my dear Bernard, is a contradiction in terms. Ha? There *is* no such thing as good Mexican food. Mexicans are poor people, and they eat only the cheapest things available." Other theories of Laszlo were that the staple foods all around the world, the foods the poorest lived on, were always soft so the very old, the very young, and the toothless could eat them. He enumerated: "Rice in China, Japan, India, most of the East; potatoes in Russia and Germany; pasta in Italy; and cheeseburgers in this country. I mean those soft, soggy ones in fast-food joints."

Bernard never argued about food with Laszlo. There were better topics for arguments with him, such as why Mozart had chosen certain keys for certain moods in his music; whether other composers had similar mental associations with keys; whether this was a matter of personal idiosyncrasy or whether there was a general underlying principle. Laszlo was always looking for underlying principles, such as the open strings used in keys like D and A making for a brilliant sound no matter who the composer was, while Bernard sought the answer in personal preference or symbolic meaning. These were not arguments in which anyone convinced anyone else, but they were fun to pursue. One could always name yet another composition to prove one's point this way or that.

When Bernard arrived at the Czech restaurant, Laszlo was sitting at the bar having a drink with a rosy-cheeked, jovial-looking fellow. The way he patted him on the back when he rose to join Bernard indicated that he was either a good friend or that Laszlo had had more than one drink.

"Do you know what that fellow told me—he's an oboist

I know from recording sessions—no, not told me, asked me? He asked do I know why Bach had so many children? You know what he said? Ha-ha-ha-ha. Because Bach had no stops on his organ."

"Oh, my God!"

This time Laszlo had laughed even before the punchline of the joke. At least it was not as long as his usual stories. They sat down, ordered dinner, and sipped a glass of wine while waiting for it to be served. Laszlo was reporting details of an amusing recording session he had been involved in that afternoon. As Bernard knew from past experience, Laszlo did not believe in discussing matters of importance while eating; he liked to devote his full attention to the delicate combinations of flavors offered. After dinner they sat in silence until the table was cleared except for a demitasse and a cognac in front of each of them.

"Bernard," he began, "do you know Mozart piano concerto in D minor? Köchel number 466, I believe. It opens a little like commendatore music from *Don Giovanni*."

"I'm acquainted with it, but I've never studied it. Doesn't the second movement, called Romanza, have lots of passages in sixteenth-note triplets?"

"It does indeed, my dear Bernard. And last movement is very energetic Rondo, one of the few rondos in minor key that Mozart wrote."

"Are most Mozart rondos in the major key? I've never thought about it."

"If you have a free hour, look around Mozart music and you will see I am right. Most of them are bright, happy pieces in major key."

"Well, this one is in the minor, though. I think I remember the main theme." Bernard hummed the opening bars.

"It's sort of balanced without being symmetrical. And it does go into the major key near the end, doesn't it?"

"It does, and I see you know the piece even if you never played it. My next question is: Would you be willing to learn it?"

"Learn it? What for?"

"I tell you what for: I always loved this concerto, so much so it made me sorry I play fiddle and not piano. I always wanted to do it with my orchestra."

"I still don't know what you are leading up to."

"You're a little slow today, my dear Bernard, slow on the uptake, as they say. All right then, here's the situation: I kept a spot open on my programs next season for you and Lydia to play Mozart two-piano concerto. When members of my board of directors read the review of your joint recital—the one I couldn't go to—they turned cool to the proposition. I cannot go against their wishes. But my board still likes *you* and your playing. They loved your appearance with us the year before. They would like you to be our soloist again."

He rose from his seat and took a bow in Bernard's direction.

"I hereby invite you most formally and officially to play Mozart D Minor Concerto with us next season. It will be sometime in March. I don't have the exact date yet."

He sat down again.

"Oh, Laszlo, I'd be delighted to play that concerto with you. It would really be something to look forward to."

"You accept my invitation? Good. Between us we shall try to do it justice. To touch a touchy subject, how's Lydia?"

"I was wondering when you'd get around to that. As you may have guessed, we don't see each other anymore. Well, that's not entirely correct: I do see her when she brings her son to me for his weekly lesson. But she never stays to listen or to talk. She drops him off and picks him up again an hour later."

"So you separated. To tell the truth, I'm not completely surprised. I always thought her love for you was somehow mixed in with your music. That doesn't mean she didn't love you for yourself. Oh, God, I think I'm talking myself into trouble here. I should shut up. This is really none of my business."

"I don't mind your talking about her, Laszlo. Actually it'll do me good. I never understood why she cut me out of her life so totally and so brutally, but she did. I've thought about it a great deal, as you can imagine, and I've come to the conclusion that success or failure was more important to her than music and I. That sounds awful, but I think it's true. It probably all began with her being a second daughter. She could not tolerate failure—even her ex-husband told me that in the one conversation I had with him—and when I became associated with failure in her mind, I had to go, I had to be cut out of her life. I still miss her, though, very badly sometimes."

"I'm sure you do. One doesn't get over things easily. The pain just diminishes little by little. I hope you're not angry with her in your memory?"

"I was at first, very angry. She didn't come to me to talk things over, as I would have expected her to do. She went on a long visit to her parents in South Carolina and sneaked back into town without calling me. I ran into her by accident at some painter's show, and she kissed that painter blatantly when she knew I was watching."

"People do strange things when they are hurt themselves. They want to hurt those who hurt them. Punish them for what they've done."

"She certainly did just that."

"Look, Bernard. Having bitter memories really doesn't help anything. Try to remember the *good* she did for you. Just before she came to you, you were telling me always that there's no excitement, no variety in your life; that all is routine and repeating itself and you have nothing to look forward to. She pulled you out from all that. Please remember! Also, as some English poet said, is better to have loved and lost than not to have loved at all."

"I know that line—it's either Tennyson or Wordsworth—and I agree with its sentiment. But it doesn't alleviate my hard feelings for Lydia."

"No, of course it doesn't, but it's true all the same. Let me tell you one more thing while we're on this topic: I'm not so sure it's a good idea to mix love with one's profession. Many years ago, soon after I came to the United States, I was member of a string quartet that toured a lot. I was second violin, and viola was a lovely girl from California. Before you knew it, we were in bed together, and not long after that we had some justice of the peace—what a wonderful title!—declare us man and wife.

"It made touring easier and much more pleasurable. We also saved a lot of money on hotel bills. But soon there were problems. How shall I explain? It began in rehearsals. If you and violist don't agree about how a certain phrase should be played, you talk it out and find solution. But if violist is your wife, it's not that simple. Every argument is carried on into bed—you know what I mean—and, what is worse, all problems of bedroom are brought into rehearsal room.

"Soon tension between her and me was so high, other members of quartet told us one of us would have to leave. Naturally I, Hungarian gentleman that I am, made first offer and they accepted. Why am I telling you all this? To show that perhaps professionally it would not have worked out with you and Lydia in the long run."

"You may be right, Laszlo, it may not have worked out for us in the long run. May I thank you for speaking so freely about your own life tonight? You have never done that before. I did not even know that you had ever been married. Thank you also for showing so much understanding and sympathy for human problems."

"That's what they call a backhanded compliment if I ever heard one. Did you really think I consist only of jokes?"

"I may have thought so at times, to be absolutely honest, but I won't anymore. As you know, musical talent doesn't always go hand in hand with other human characteristics like intelligence or compassion. Musical talent falls wherever God chooses to put it."

"Let's not get philosophical or sentimental now, Bernard, the cognac is too good for that. Are you seeing anyone else, or am I being indiscreet?"

"I do not intend to spend the rest of my life in celibacy. I was not made for that. Yes, I'm seeing a very pleasant young woman named Felicia Weissman. We get along very well together—in all respects—but it is more of a convenience than a great passion. We both know it will end one day, but in the meantime we enjoy each other."

"Is she musician?"

"No, but she knows and loves music. Could I go out with anyone who doesn't? Her husband—they're separated but not divorced and on decent terms with each other—is very well-to-do and interested in the theater. Before becoming an investment banker he wanted to go on the stage. Now he supports small independent groups who put on experimental plays and employ struggling young actors. Naturally he's beset by applications, and Felicia helps him sort out genuine talent from frauds. She goes to see their performances to find out whether they deserve support or not. Sometimes I go with her to dingy little halls where ill-clad young people put on plays in front of empty seats. What they get paid, if they get paid at all, is ludicrous, and yet they all want to be there, to act, to be on stage. Perhaps they hope to be discovered by some talent scout."

"No doubt they do. And yet I see much idealism in these young people. They are more interested in theater than in material things like cars, clothes, and all the paraphernalia of the 'upwardly mobile.'"

"You do see the good in everything, Laszlo. God bless you."

"I asked you not to get philosophical or sentimental. Please stick to it."

"Sorry if I seem to be carrying on. There's a bitterness in me that vents itself on seemingly innocent objects. I'll have to learn to control it."

"It'll go away one day. Very soon, I hope. Now, what about Lydia's son? You always talked about him a lot."

"He continues to amaze me. I've never taught children before, as you know. To watch a child grow in front of your eyes, faster than any adult would, is something new for me. And what a pleasure it is! Carl is no run-of-the-mill child, either. He has talent, energy, willpower, and an inborn understanding of music. He may turn out to be another Roger; his potential is even greater."

"I'm glad your enthusiasm hasn't diminished. That's quite a list of qualities you gave that boy. My board of directors has been talking about having an annual competition for young performers; piano one year, violin or cello the next, the winner to play a concerto with my orchestra. When the time comes, perhaps Lydia's son would be interested."

"Contests and competitions! I've quite a song to sing about them, Laszlo. You may not want to hear it. They all focus on success and failure."

"Funny you should put it this way, *singing* about success and failure. I once conducted a piece by a young composer that did just that. It was for soprano and chamber orchestra, single winds. And the text! I'll never forget it. It was by Emily Dickinson, and the composer repeated the opening line several times. If I sing the tune, the words will come back to me. This is how it went."

Laszlo began to sing in a surprisingly high-pitched voice. Perhaps he was imitating the soprano. He sang:

> Success is counted sweetest
> tara, tara, tara
> By those who don't succeed;
> tari, tari, tara
> To comprehend a nectar
> Requires sorest need.

"The composer never repeated the other two lines," he went on. "They must have had less meaning for him. I'm not sure I understand them either. But those first two lines: 'Success is counted sweetest by those who don't succeed.' Don't they sum it all up? I hope I am quoting exactly.

"Now to return to our topic in earnest: I strongly believe contests are the best way to discover unusual talent. To win a contest takes endurance and stamina, qualities needed for career in music. Don't you think so? If I had not won competition in Budapest when I was small boy, I might never have become musician at all."

The Music Teacher

"Contests are decided by judges," Bernard countered. "Their prejudices, even their phobias, influence their decisions. Contests will always be the most blatant, the most obvious, the most visible juxtaposition of success and failure."

"Look, Bernard. Some things can be divided up, others cannot. There are many situations in life, from presidency of country to piano contest in small town, where there can be only *one* winner. All others must be losers, whether they are behind by a huge or a tiny margin. Ever since I have known you, Bernard, you have ranted on and on about success and failure. Why is it so important to you?"

Bernard suddenly noticed how quiet it had become around them. He looked up and saw that they were the last guests left in the restaurant. All the other tables had been cleared and were already set up for the next day's lunch. Someone had dimmed the lights, and a waiter hovered near them without any apparent reason.

It had not escaped Laszlo either.

"Let's get out of here," he said, "before they kick us out. As you know, nothing lasts forever, not this dinner, not your affair with Lydia, not even Mozart's Concerto in D Minor."

He rose from his seat

"But before we leave, let me tell you something with all the strength of my conviction. You are a very successful teacher of music, Bernard, a *very* successful teacher indeed, and that is no small achievement. Where would Roger be without you? Where would Lydia's young son be without you? Where, in fact, would music be tomorrow without you and others like you?"

His resonant voice could be heard all over the restaurant. Two of the waiters were listening with interest. Laszlo put his hand on Bernard's shoulder and, with a smile that slowly turned into a benevolent but knowing grin, he whispered in his ear, "And as far as women are concerned, my dear Bernard, you're good at getting them—quite a success—but not so good at keeping them. Isn't that so?"

Laszlo is really a good friend, Bernard told himself as he walked toward his car, and he is certainly not a fool. He said some wise words this evening, especially the ones about mixing one's profession with one's love life. And yet I have done it twice, and twice I ended up alone. Should I have married the biblical type of "good" woman? She would have been content to cook, keep me sane and safe, and say on the telephone, "He's busy, but I will give him your message." I looked for other qualities in a companion.

What is it then? Is it really only that Mitzi had too much success with her music and Lydia too little? It can't be that simple. Is there something in me that has turned them away? He thought of his mother's Goethe quote about living *with* someone and living *in* someone. Did I fail in this regard? If living in someone meant understanding them, I certainly tried, even if I did not succeed. Did I injure or harm them in a way I was not aware of? Certainly not Mitzi, but perhaps Lydia. She did say so at one point. Will I ever know?

"Life is too long to be spent with one person," he had read somewhere recently. Did I want to spend the rest of my life with Lydia? Did I perhaps overestimate her musical ability when I pushed her toward a career?

As he opened his car door, he suddenly remembered a sentence his old lady teacher had used on her students often: "Don't go into music for money or fame," she had said. "Do it only if music means more to you than anything else in the world."

He closed the car door and sat thinking for a moment.

The Music Teacher

Yes, he said to himself, music will be the rest of my life. There will probably be other women—I was not meant to be celibate—but none will have as much importance to me as music. To deepen my knowledge of musical works I have known for many years (in really great musical works you discover new things every time you study them again, as he had often told his students), to learn new pieces and through them to meet new musical minds, and, finally (no need to be modest about it), to help others see the beauty and the meaning of serious music—in other words: to teach—that will be the rest of my life. Yes. Music, yes.

As he began to drive, he found himself humming in a low voice, but with a clearly defined rhythm, a repetitive motif to the words "Music, yes." What an ostinato, he thought: two sixteenths notes, a rest, and an off-beat eighth. As the car gathered speed, the tune became louder and more intense.

3/10